William Pain

Practical Builder

Workman's General Assistant

William Pain

Practical Builder
Workman's General Assistant

ISBN/EAN: 9783337375980

Printed in Europe, USA, Canada, Australia, Japan

Cover: Foto ©Andreas Hilbeck / pixelio.de

More available books at **www.hansebooks.com**

THE
PRACTICAL BUILDER,

O R

WORKMAN's GENERAL ASSISTANT:

Shewing the moſt approved and eaſy METHODS for DRAWING and
WORKING the whole or ſeparate PART of any BUILDING, as

The Uſe of the TRAMEL for GROINS, ANGLE - BRACKETS, NICHES, &c.

Semi-circular ARCHES on Flewing JAMBS, the preparing and making their SOFFITS.

RULES OF CARPENTRY;

To find the LENGTH and BACKING of HIPS, ſtrait or curved; TRUSSES for ROOFS,
DOMES, &c.——Truſſing of GIRDERS, SECTIONS of FLOORS, &c.

The Proportion cf the Five Orders, in their general and particular Parts, Gluing of Columns,
STAIR-CASES with their *ramp* and *twiſt* RAILS, fixing the CARRIAGES, NEWELS, &c.

Frontiſpieces, Chimney-Pieces, Ceilings, Cornices, Architraves, &c. in the neweſt Taſte.

With Plans and Elevations of Gentlemens and Farm-Houſes, Yards, Barns, &c.

By WILLIAM PAIN, ARCHITECT and JOINER.

Engraved on Eighty-three PLATES.

LONDON: PRINTED for I. TAYLOR, at the BIBLE and CROWN, in
HOLBORN, near CHANCERY-LANE,
MDCCLXXIV.

PREFACE.

COnsidering the Number of Books on the Theory and Practice of Architecture already published, any further Effort to illustrate and familiarize this MOST NOBLE ART, may seem superfluous and unnecessary; in me especially, who, by two former Publications, endeavoured to advance the young Practitioner in the Knowledge of his Profession.

But as Art is improving, greater Experience enables to discern the truly useful, and thereby to confirm or reject former Methods.

The very great Revolution (as I may say) which of late has so generally prevailed in the Stile of Architecture, especially in the decorative and ornamental Department, will evince the Necessity and eminent Utility of this Publication. That Taste (so conspicuous in our modern Buildings) which is vainly sought in any other practical Treatise, the Workman will here find illustrated in a great Variety of useful and elegant Examples.

The Deficiencies and confined Plans of those Books now used by Workmen, is another Inducement to collect together in one View, the most easy and certain Rules to carry on the Building Art. These are the Result of Experience, and by the Author long used in conducting Business, who now offers the Public a general practical Treatise, wherein his great Care has been plainly and faithfully to answer the Purpose of the manual Artificer: It is not meant to instruct the professed Artist, but to furnish the Ignorant, the Uninstructed, with such a comprehensive System of Practice, as may lay a Foundation for their Improvement, and thereby enable them to execute with Ease and Precision, the various Branches of the Profession.

THE
TABLE of CONTENTS.

A *TABLE* for the Cutting of Timber for Building.

Bearing Poſt.

Height.	
If 8 Feet	9 Inch. ſquare
— 10 —	10 by 9
— 12 —	11 — 12
— 16 —	14 — 15
— 20 —	16 — 18

Girder's Bearing.

If 10 Feet	10 by 9 In.
— 12 —	11 — 10
— 14 —	12 — 11
— 16 —	12 — 13
— 18 —	13 — 14
— 20 —	15 — 14
— 24 —	15 — 16
— 30 —	16 — 18

Binding Joiſts.

Bearing	Inches
6 Feet	6 by 4
8 —	7 — 4
9 —	8 — 4
12 —	10 — 5

Bridging Joiſts.

Whoſe Bearing ſhould not exceed 5 Feet, and Scantling not leſs than 6 by 4.

Common Joiſt.

Bearing	Inches
6 Feet	6 by 3
9 —	9 — 3
12 —	12 — 4

Beams or Ties.

Length	Inches
12 Feet	7 by 8
16 —	8 — 9
20 —	9 — 10
30 —	10 — 11
40 —	12 — 11
50 —	13 — 12

Small Rafters.

Bearing	Inches
8 Feet	5 by 3
10 —	7 — 3
12 —	8 — 4

Principal Rafters.

Length	Boᵗᵐ. Top. Thick.
From 12 to 16 Feet	8 — 6 — 5
From 16 to 20 —	9 — 7 — 6
From 23 to 24 —	10 — 8 — 7
From 24 to 30 —	12 — 10 — 9

Purlins from 8 by 5 to 9 by 7 or 10 by 8.

Raiſing Plates from 7 by 5 to 8 by 6, or 10 by 8.

Ground-fills the ſame as Raiſing Plates.

To face PLATE I.

Figure *A* and *B* are ribb'd NICHES for Plaistering.

THE Plan *a* is a Semi-Elipsis on the tranfverfe Diameter, which is drawn with a Tramel as reprefented in the Plan, which is to be made with a Grove at Right Angles as in the Figure ; two Pieces to be morticed to flip on the Rod, and one fixed at the End for a Pencil, &c. fix one of the Pieces equal to half the Conjugate Diameter, and the other to half the Tranfverfe Diameter, and moving the Rod with the Pins in the Groves, the Pencil will defcribe the Semi-Elipfis.

To draw the Elipfis *c* to any given Length and Breadth, take half the Conjugate Diameter *a b* and fet it on the Tranfverfe Diameter *d c* divide *c a* into three equal Parts, and make *c e* equal to one of thofe Parts, and with the Radius *e f* bifect *g g*. So the Points *e f* and *g g* are the Centres for drawing the Elipfis to any Length and Breadth.

To draw the Elipfis *d* with a Line, take half the Tranfverfe Diameter *b a* and fet it from *c* on the Conjugate Diameter to *d* on the Tranfverfe Diameter, and to *e* on ditto, then *e d* are the Points to be fixed for the Line to go round, which will defcribe the E-lipfis with the Point *f*.

To glue the Head of a Nich as Figure *e*, cut the Arch Part of the Board or Stave to the Thicknefs of a Veneer, and bend it on a Templet, and back it to the Curve, it may be jointed the fame as a Column, &c.

To defcribe a Polygon to a given Side from five to eight Sides, make a Radius of the given Side for the Pentagon, divide the Arch into five Parts, turn one down on the Line which is the Centre, to defcribe a Circle which will contain the Side five Times.

For a Hexagon, the Radius of the Side is the Centre.

The Heptagon into feven Parts and turn one up.

The Octagon into four and turn one up.

To raife a Perpendicular at the End or Middle of a Line. Defcribe the Arch *c d*, and with the Radius *a c* make *e f*, which bifect at *b*, gives the Perpendicular to *a*.

To let fall a Perpendicular from a given Point to a Bafe Line. Figure *G*; let *a* be the Point given to fall to the Bafe Line *b c*, draw a right Line from *a* at pleafure to meet the Bafe Line as at *c*, more or lefs; divide the Line *c a* into two Parts, and draw the Semi-Circle *a b c*, and where the Circle cuts the Bafe Line at *b*, which is at Right Angles with *a*, which was to be done.

Plate I.

Niches, Polygons, Framels &c.

The Framel Rod

B

A

Conjugal Diameter

Transverse Diameter

D

C

E

Octagon

Heptagon

Hexagon

Pentagon

A Framel to strike a Segment or Flat Arch

G

F

The Arch line of a, Stretched out at lenght.

Fig. O, is a Ribbid Nich for plaistering with the Ribs all joind to ý place where to stand the Edges are Bevel so the mould must be shifted.

The arch line of b. Stretched out at lenght.

Fig. F. is a plan of Nich to be fincered H, is the fincer stretched out at lenght from ý Arch I. & 2 F, is ý plan which ý edges are traced from which is plain to Inspect but the more parts it is divided into the truer the Round the plan is in 7 parts but in practice it may be into 15 parts or more at pleasure.

Fig. A, is a Plan of a Cellar Ground in B & C are the Sections which shew how the hip is traced to make the Angle streight over ý plan D and E, are the covering or face of the Groins stretched out from which a mould may be made to make the hip or Angle streight if the Ribs C, O, are set first & boarded in the mould must be taken from E, but if the Arches in Section B, be set first the mould must be taken from D.

Plate III.

Fig. B. is an Arch standing on Fleming Jambs in a Straight Wall
and supposed to be a fair Arch in Stone or Brick.
Divide the Round of the Arch in as many Parts as are Courses
to Compleat the Arch and drop them to the Wall Line, then
Draw them cross the Wall, Parallel with the Jambs, and
that shews how much is to be Cutt of the Face of each
Course.

Circular Arches &c.
in a Circular Wall.

Fig. A. is a Circular Wall which
has a Door or Window that
stands Fleming. Because the Jambs
do not stand at Right Angles
with the Diameter of the Circle, as
in Plate IV find the Curve Line
of the Soffit. in this Case draw the
Cord Line or Base Line of the
Arch o, g at Right Angles with
the Jambs o. k to touch the Arch
of the Wall at a, and Divide the
Arch into equal Parts and drop
them to the Wall then take of
the Distances. h. g. 8. g. 7. i. 6. k.
&c. and put them on the Arch
stretched out. Gives the edge
of the Soffit.

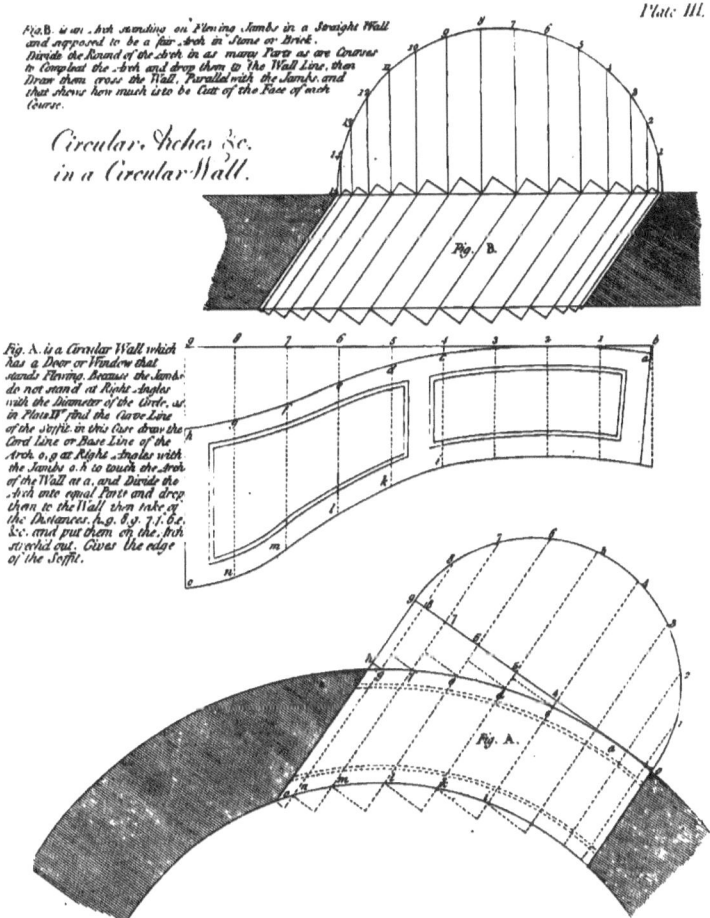

Fig. B.

Fig. A.

To face PLATE IV.

Figure *A* is a PLAN to be GROIN'D.

DIVIDE the Bafe Line *a* of the given Rib into equal Parts, and that of *d* into the fame Number of Parts, and draw Lines to the Arch Line of *a*, and likewife in *d* at pleafure; then take 1, 2, 3, 4, 5, 6, &c. from *a*, and transfer them to *d*, as 1, 2, 3, 4, 5, 6, &c. and thro' the Point 1, 2, 4, 6, 8; trace the Arch Line over *d*, and fo for the Reft, as is plain to Infpection. The Angle Bracket is done in the fame Manner.

To defcribe a Circular Soffit in a Circular Wall, as in *B*. Draw the Cord Line of the Arch, or Bafe Line fo called, to touch the Arch of the Wall, then draw the Semi-Circle and divide the Round of it in a Number of equal Parts as here into 9, but the more Parts the truer the Work, and draw them to the Arch of the Wall, then ftretch out the Arch Line at Length as in *e*, and transfer the Parts that are between the Wall and Bafe Line, as 1, 2, 3, 4, 5, 6, &c. to *e*, which gives the Edge of the Soffit or Pannel.

To defcribe a Circular Soffit in a ftrait Wall on flewing Jambs. Continue the flewing of the Wall till it meets at *b*, then fet the Compaffes at *b*, and draw two Arches to the Thicknefs of the Wall, then put on the Girt of the Soffit *c d*, which gives the Length of the Soffit and Edge of ditto.

Plate IV.

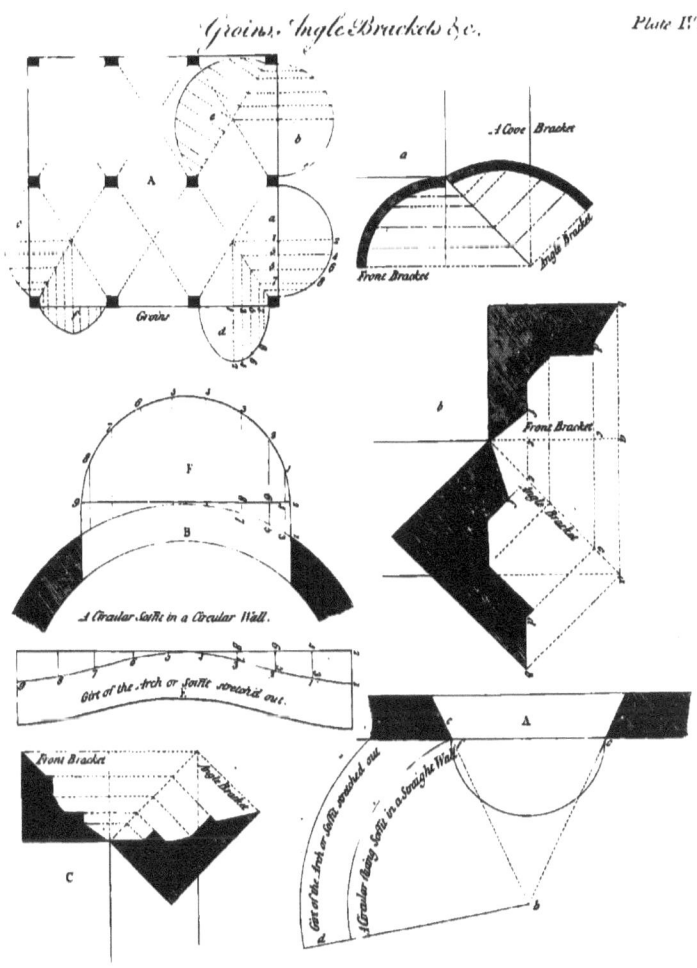

A

Groins

A Cove Bracket

a

Front Bracket

Ingle Bracket

Front Bracket

Ingle Bracket

b

F

B

A Circular Soffit in a Circular Wall.

Girt of the Arch or Soffit stretched out.

Front Bracket

Angle Bracket

C

A

Girt of the Arch or Soffit stretched out

A Circular Rising Soffit in a Straight Wall.

b

Plate V.

Trussing Girders Floors &c.

The Dovetail to have one Inch and Quarter Draft on each Side the Beam.

The Girder to be Cutt one Inch Camber in 20 Foot &c. notwithstanding they are to be Truss'd

The Truss to be of Dry Oak about 4 inches Square, to have Iron Plates at the Ends & Meetings.

Truss Partition

Girder

Girder

Binding Joist

Binding Joist

Section of a Bridge Floor

Section of a Floor with the Binding Joist the whole Depth.

Note: All Floors that are more than a Foot in Depth should be Bridged.

with three Joists in the interval between the Binding framd into the Girders the same way with Binding Joists but not so Deep as ditto as a.b.c. &c.

These sort of Floors not to be more than a Foot in Depth.

Curb Roof.

To face P L A T E VI.

Figure *A.* Plan and Ledgment of a Roof, fhewing how to find the Length and Backing of Hips, Valley, &c.

TO find the Length, take the Bafe Line of the Hips *a b*, *b c*, and *b e*, and fet them on the Bafe Line of the principal Rafters, as *b a*, *b c*, *b e*, and draw Lines from the Top of the Rafter to *a c e*, which is the Length of each Hip. Or the Length may be found by fetting up the Perpendicular from the Bafe Line of the Hips, as *b g*, and draw the Line *g a*, is the Length of the Hip. To Back the Hip, lay down the Thicknefs of the Hip at the Angle of the Plan, as *H*, and draw Lines to range the Plates, will fhew how much Wood is to come off in the Backing; that is, the Mould muft be a Piece of Wood as thick as the intended Hip, and cut it to the Splay or Pitch of the Hip at the Foot, fetting it on the Angle of the Plate in the Direction of the Hip, mark it under by the Side of the Plate; gives the true Backing in any Cafe required. A very fure and fafe Way for the Backing.

Figure *B* is the Plan of an M Roof, with Hip and Valley in Ledgment, &c.

Note, The Back of the Hip is found another Way, as in the Plan *A.* by drawing a Line at Right Angles, crofs the Bafe Line of the Hip, as *r d g*, or on any Part of the Bafe Line, and fet one Foot of the Compafs at *d*, and extend to the neareft Part of the Hip *g a*, and turn it on the Bafe Line, as at *r*, then draw the Lines from the Point *r* to *g r*, on the Edge of the Plate, which is the Backing of the Hip required. This will do in any Cafe, fquare or bevel.

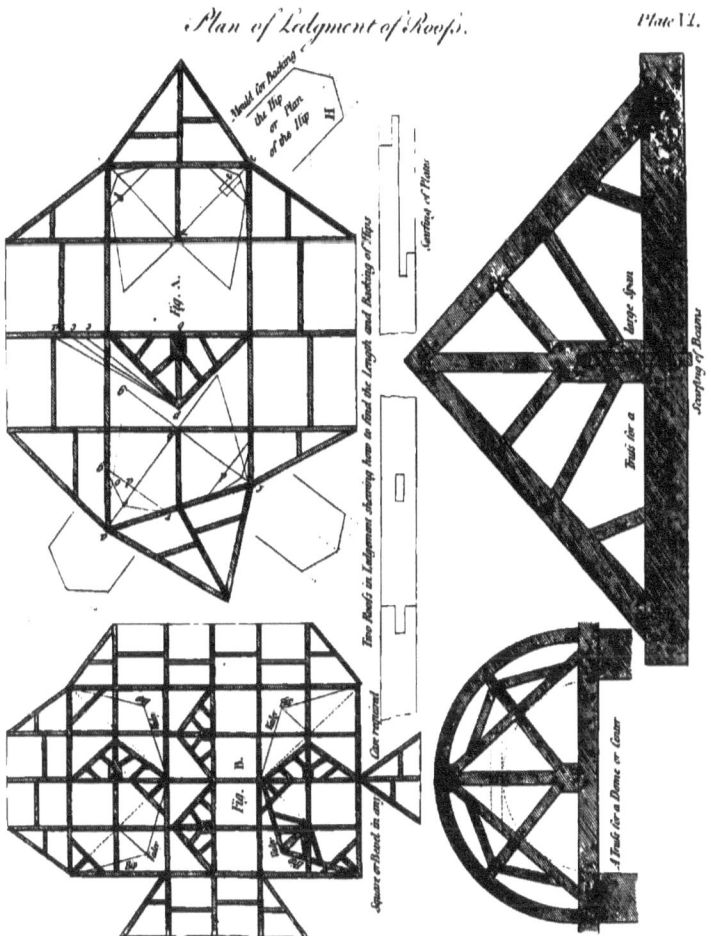

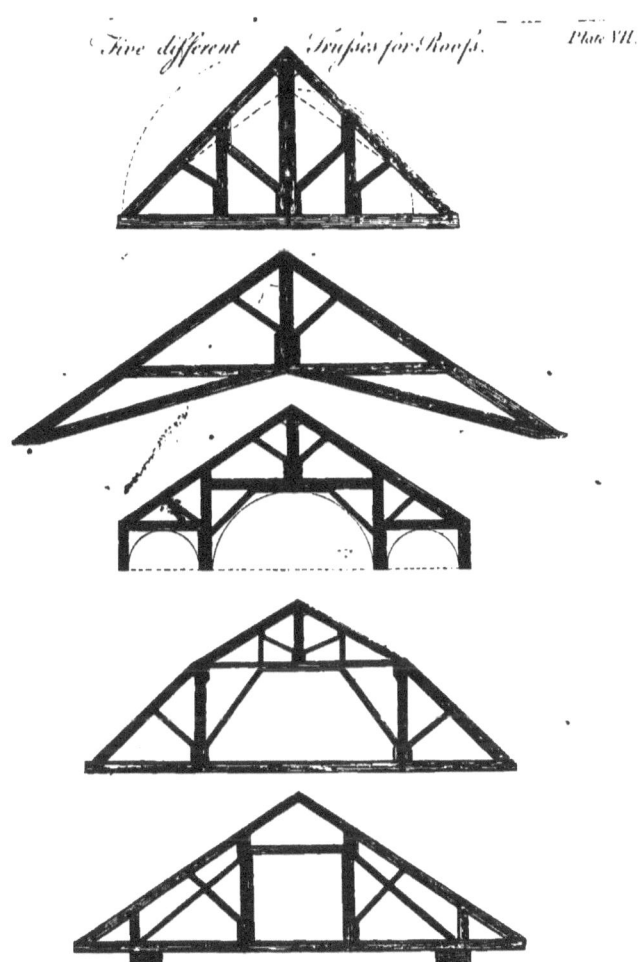

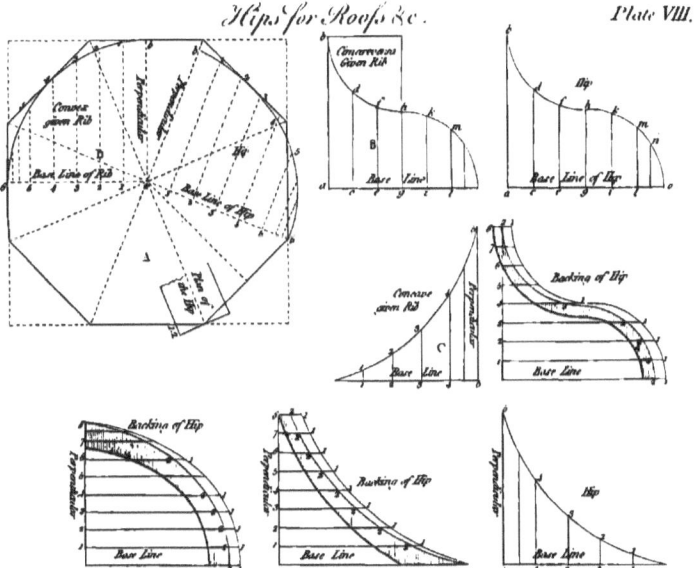

To face PLATE IX.

Truffes for the Domes of Churches, &c.

A. Is a Trufs for a Dome, with a Lanthorn or Cupola at the Top, to give Light. B. the Plan ; the Kirb or Plate to be in two Thickneffes, which is likewife beft for the Ribs, and for the Kirb on which the Cupola ftands. The Curve of the Dome A. is a Semi-circle, or will ferve for a Semi-elipfis. The Moulds f and c in the Plan B, cut the Sweep of the Purlines; and the Moulds b a and c d are for the Top and Bottom of the Purlines. C. is a Cone or Lanthorn to light a Stair-Cafe, &c. the horizontal Bars muft be fquared in the fame Manner as the Purlines in A. The Mould for cutting or fquaring the Purlines, is like the bottom Mould f in B. fo that if the Purlines be cut to the Thicknefs required as in the Section A, and alfo to the Mould f, then a is the Mould for the Bottom and b for the Top, as appears by the Lines let fall to the Plan B from the Purlines g and h ; then C in the Plan is the Top and d the bottom Mould. l is the fweep Mould for the Top of the Purline h. By this Rule the Purlines may be fquared, which completes the Work. If the Plan B, the Ribs and Purlines are in Size and Number, as the Cone C, it will do for a Lanthorn or Light to a Stair-Cafe, &c. the Manner of fquaring the Ribs and Crofs Bars is the fame as the Dome.

Plate IX.

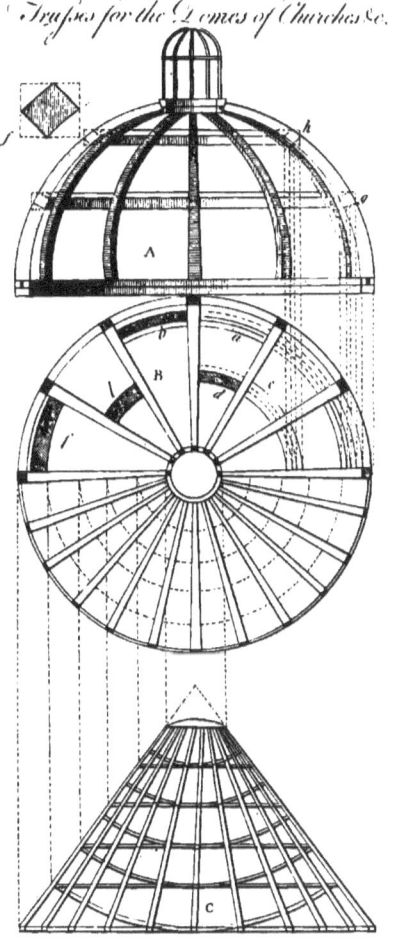

Plate X.

Mouldings, Balustrades &c.

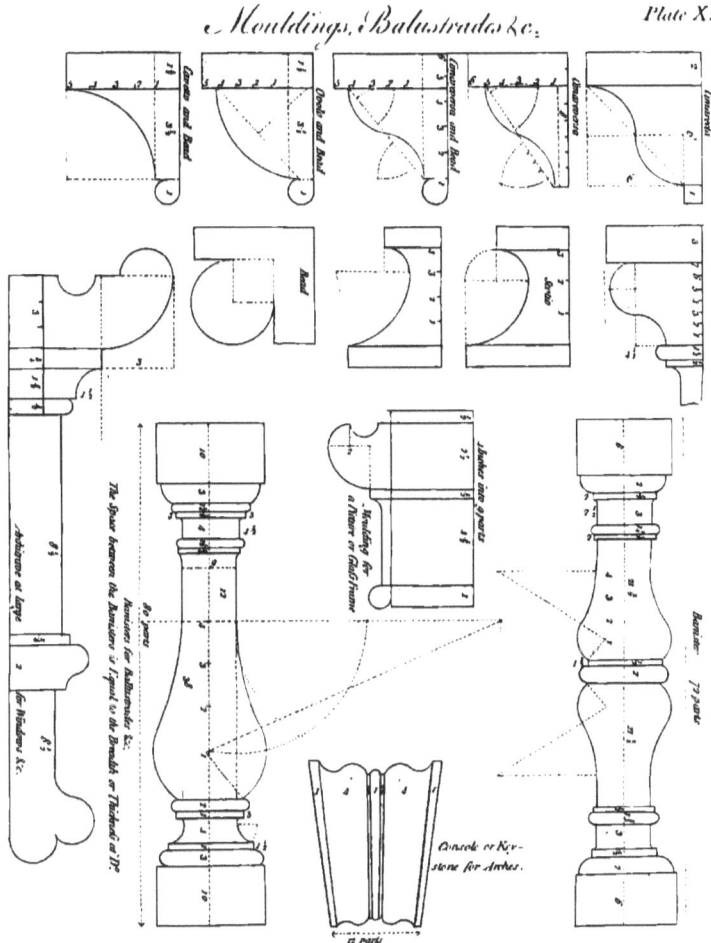

Plate XI

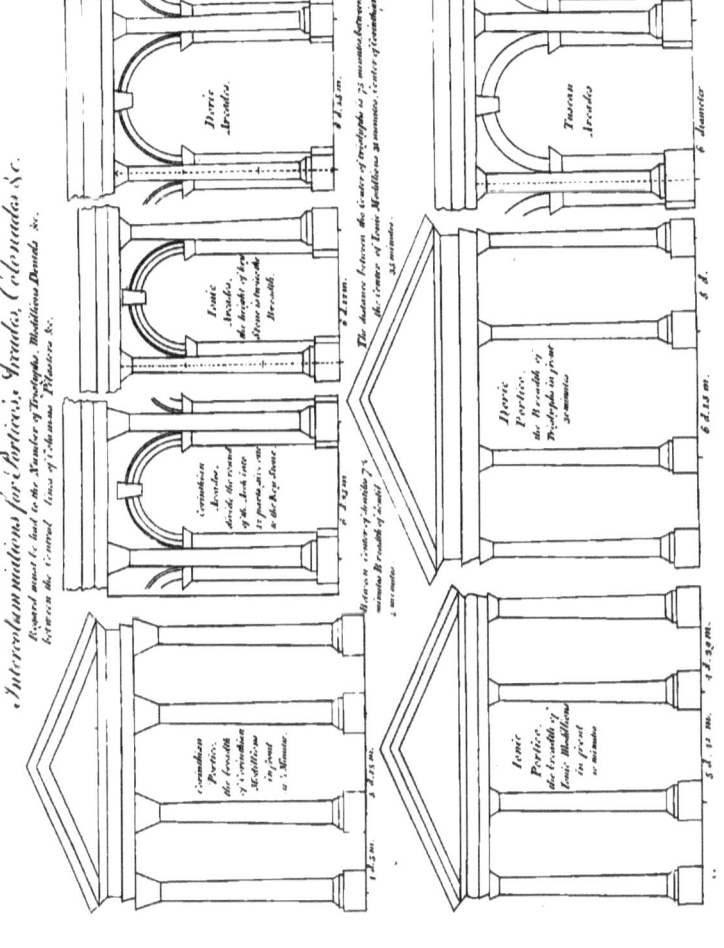

Intercolumniations for Porticos, Arcades, Colonnades &c.

Regard must be had to the Number of Tryglyphs, Modillions Dentels &c. between the Central lines of Columns Pilasters &c.

The distance between the Center of tryglyphs is 75 minutes between the Center of Ionic Modillions 30 minutes, center of Corinthian 22 minutes.

Doric Arcades

Ionic Arcades, the height of Piers to be two thirds the Breadth.

Corinthian Arcades divide the round of the Arch into 11 parts, allow one to the Key Stone.

Tuscan Arcades

Doric Portico, the Breadth of Tryglyphs in front 30 minutes.

Corinthian Portico, the Breadth of Corinthian Modillions in front 22 Minutes.

Ionic Portico, the Breadth of Ionic Modillions in front 30 minutes.

Plate XII

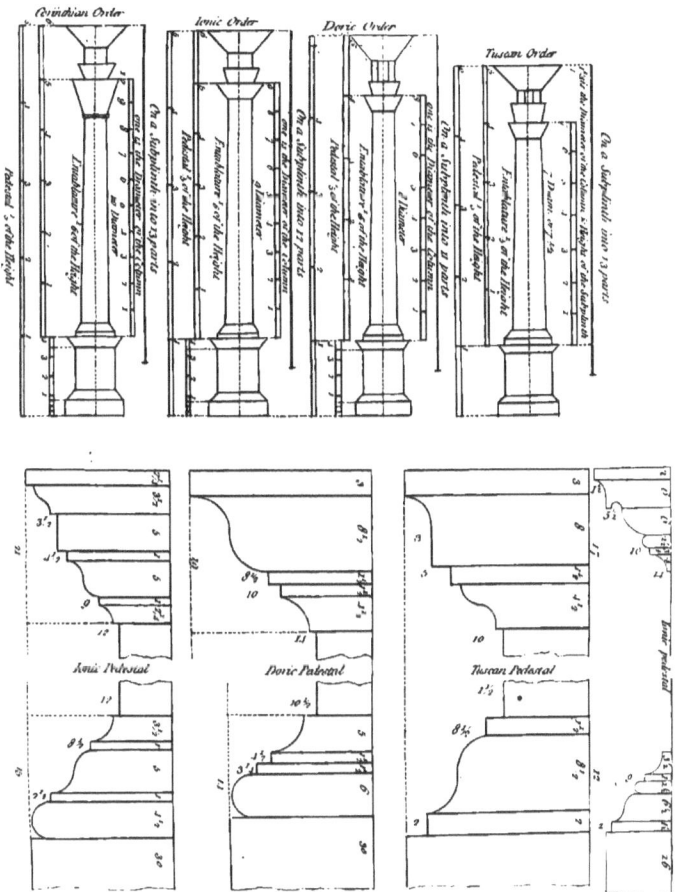

Plate XIII.

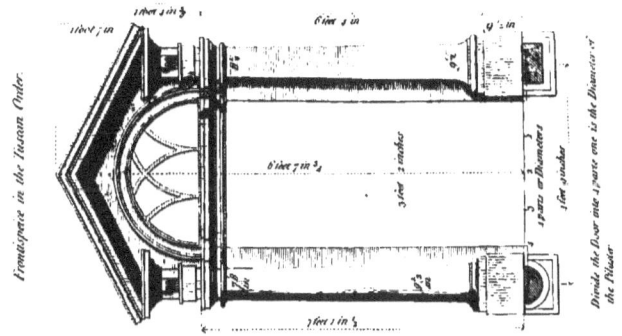

Frontispiece in the Tuscan Order.

1 feet 7 in ½   *1 feet 1 in ½*   *6 in 4 in*   *9 ½ in*

6 feet 7 in 2 ¾   *3 feet 2 inches*

Divide the Door into 4 parts one is the Diameter of the Pilaster

1 part 9 inches   *1 feet 9 inches*

1 feet 1 in ½

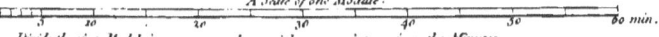

A Scale of one Module.

5   10   20   30   40   50   60 min.

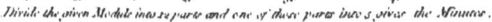

Divide the given Module into 12 parts and one of those parts into 5 gives the Minutes.

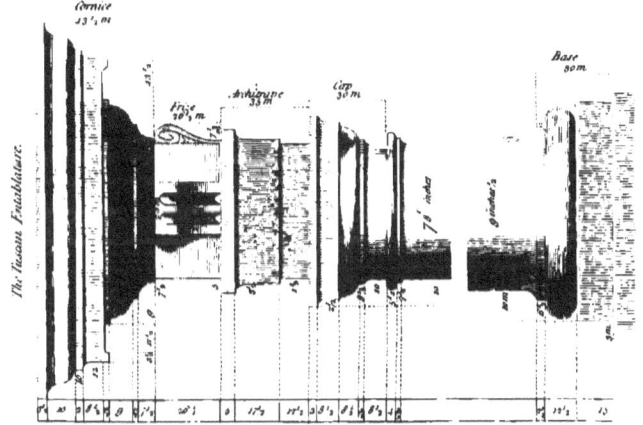

The Tuscan Entablature.

Cornice *13 ½ m*   *Frise 10 ½ m*   *Architrape 33 m*   *Capp 30 m*   *Base 30 m*

Plate XIV.

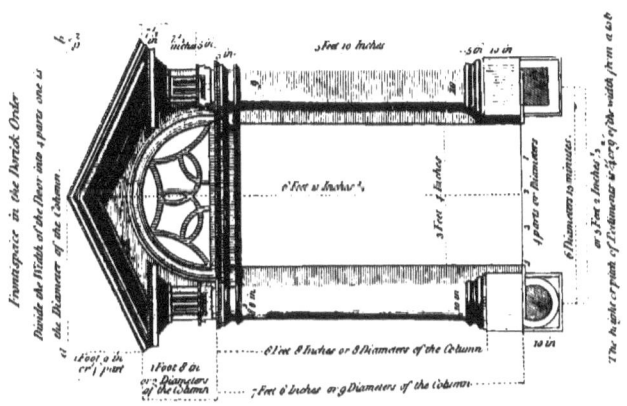

Frontispiece in the Dorick Order

Divide the Width of the Door into 4 parts one is the Diameter of the Column.

7 Inch 8 in   3 Feet 10 Inches   5 in   10 in

6 Feet 10 Inches

3 Feet 5 Inches

The whole or point of Columns is ⅔ of the width form it sett

or 3 Feet 1 Inch ; 3

6 Diameters or minutes

4 parts or Diameters

10 in

1 Foet 10 in or ¼ part

1 Foot 8 in or 2 Diameters of the Column

6 Feet 8 Inches or 5 Diameters of the Column

7 Feet 6 Inches or 9 Diameters of the Column

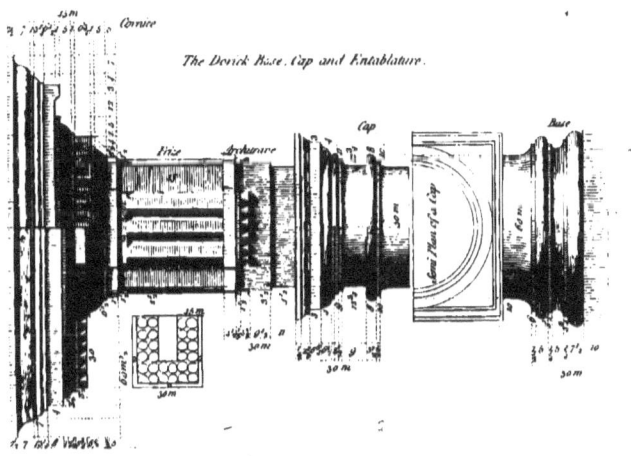

The Dorick Base, Cap and Entablature.

Cornice

Frize   Architrave   Cap   Base

Plate XV.

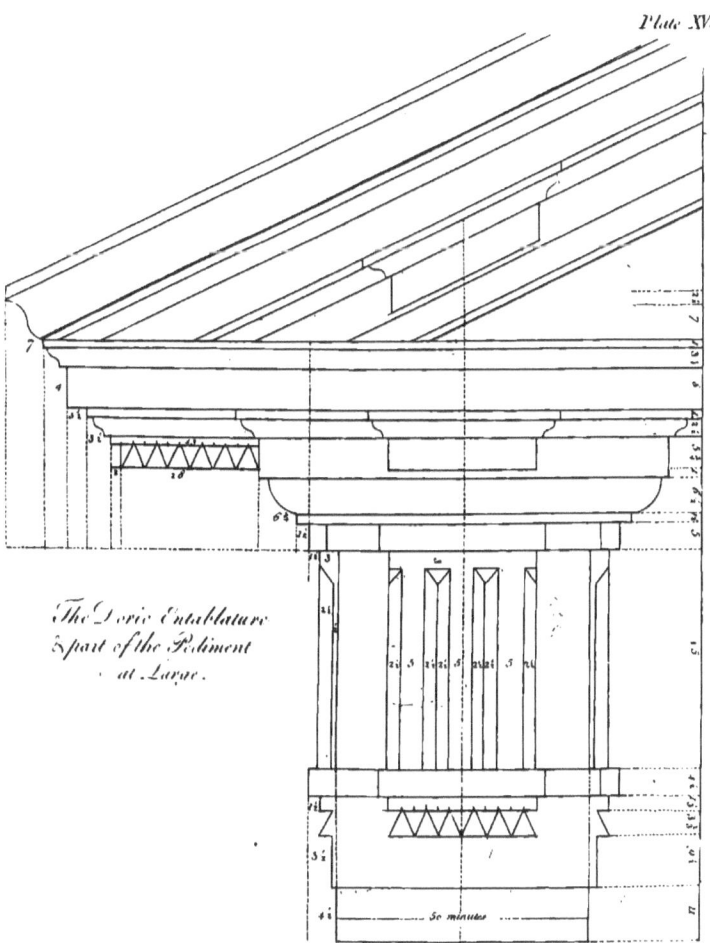

The Doric Entablature
& part of the Pediment
at Large.

Plate XVI.

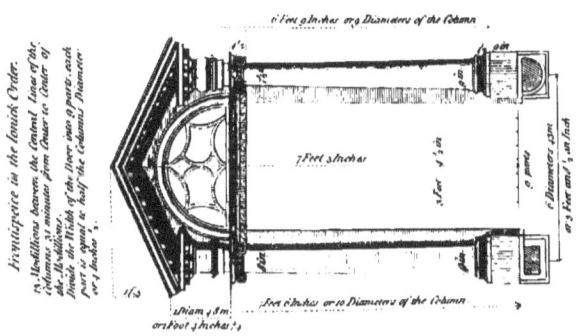

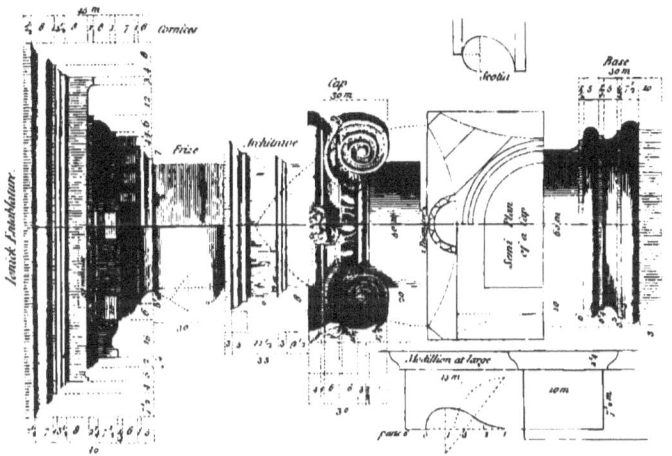

Plate XVII.

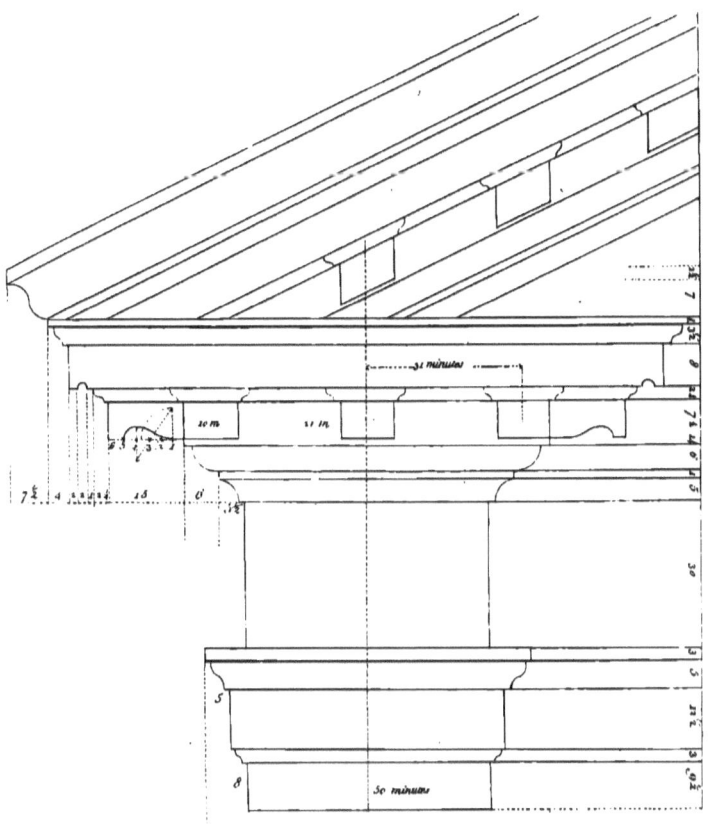

The Ionic Entablature with part of the Pediment at Large.

Plate XVIII

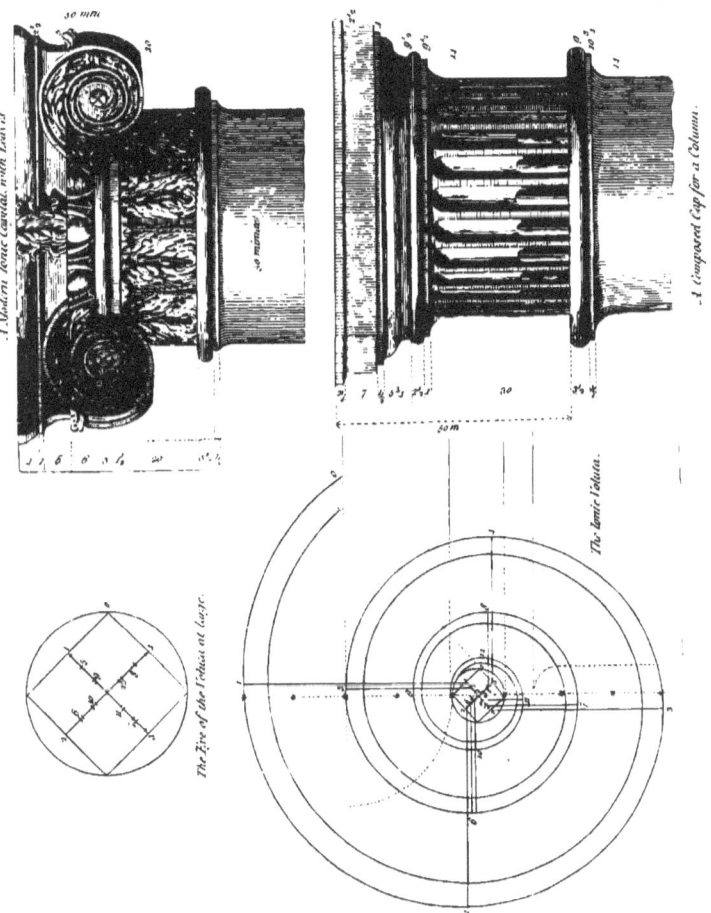

A Modern Ionic Capital, with Leaves

A Composed Cap for a Column.

The Ionic Voluta.

The Eye of the Voluta at large.

Plate XIX.

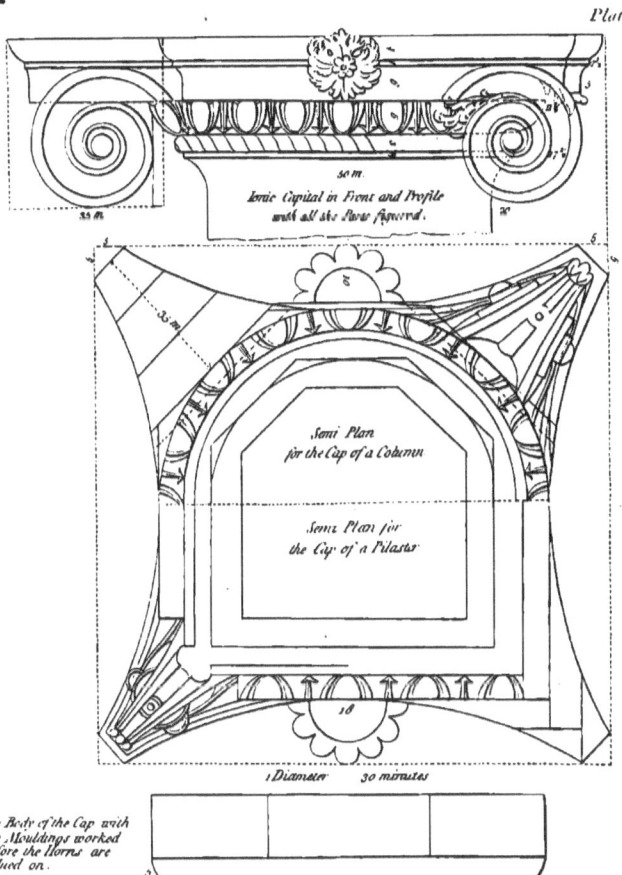

so m.

*Ionic Capital in Front and Profile
with all the Parts figured.*

33 m.

*Semi Plan
for the Cap of a Column*

*Semi Plan for
the Cap of a Pilaster*

1 Diameter   30 minutes

The Body of the Cap with
the Mouldings worked
before the Horns are
Glued on.

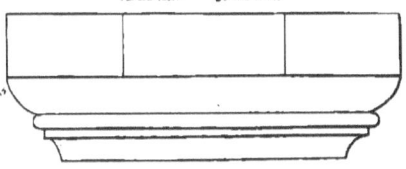

Plate XX.

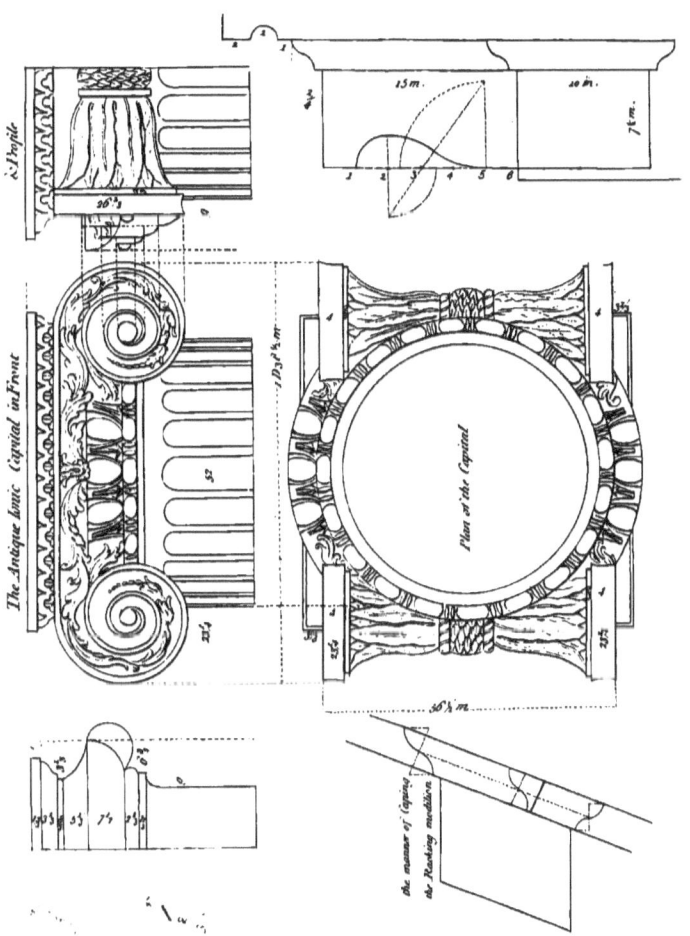

The Antique Ionic Capital in Front

Profile

Plan of the Capital

the manner of Capping the Racking moulding

Plate XXI.

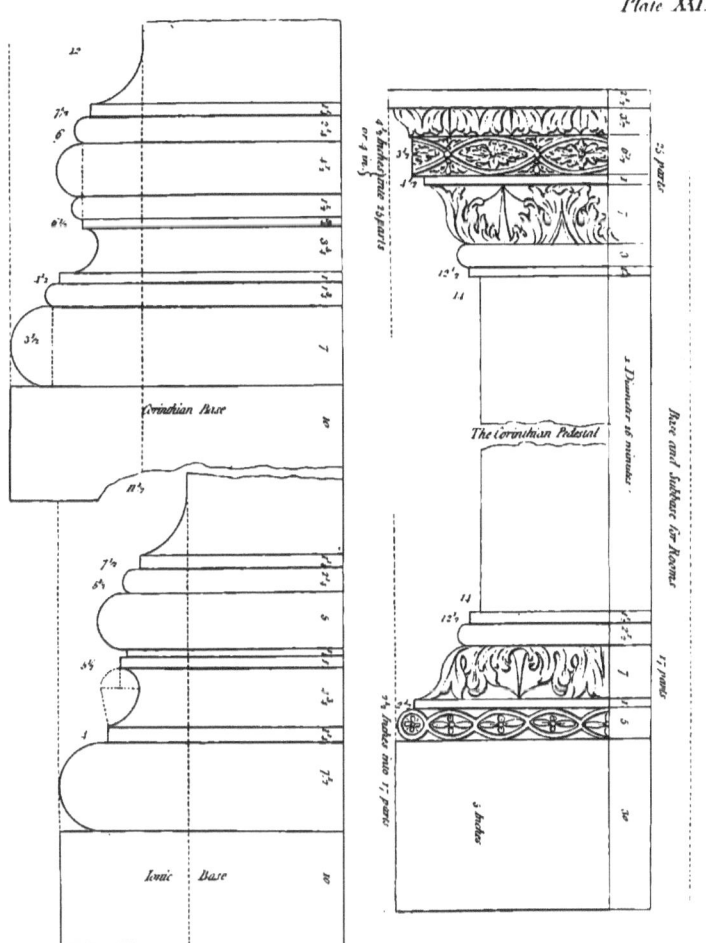

Place XXII.

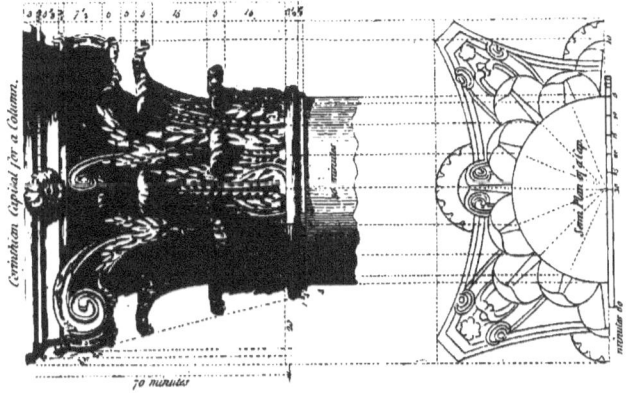

Corinthian Capital for a Column.

70 minutes

Geometrical Plan of a Vase

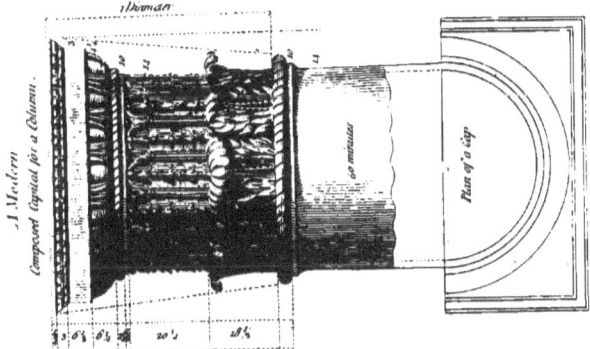

A Modern Composed Capital for a Column.

Tuscan

60 minutes

Plan of a Vase

Plate XXIII

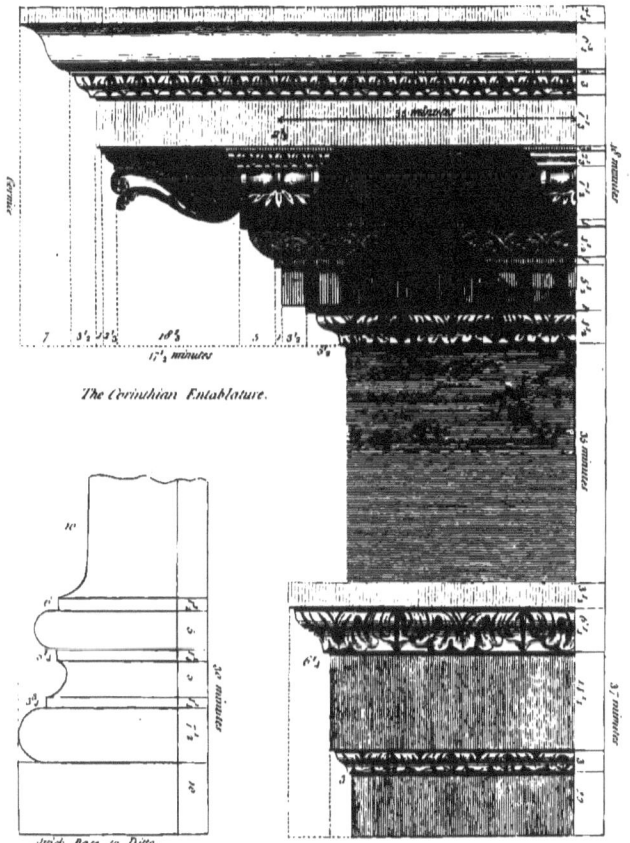

The Corinthian Entablature.

Attick Base to Ditto.

Plate XXIIII

The Antient Composite or Roman Capital

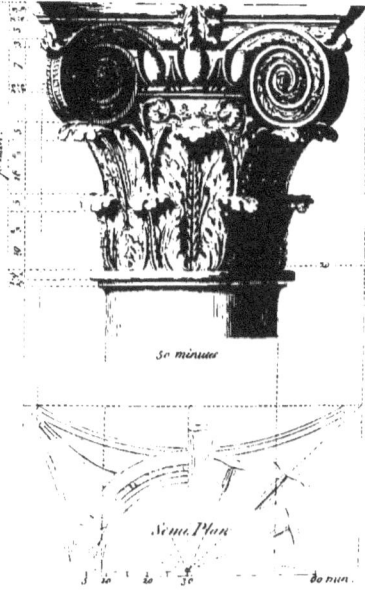

So minutes

Semi Plan

The Proportions of Composite Entablature are
the same as the Corinthian.

may be used with the Attic Base.

Plate XXVI.

Plancier of the Corinthian Cornice at an External Angle.   Plancier of the Ionic Cornice at an External Angle.

Plancier of the Doric Cornice at an External Angle.

Plate XXVII.

Gluing of Columns.

This Column Diminishes from one third of the Height.

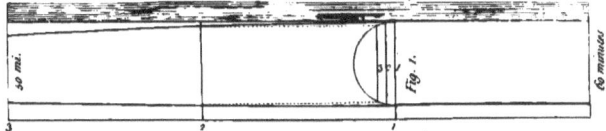

The manner of Glueing up Columns & Diminishing them

This Column Diminishes from the Bottom to the Top

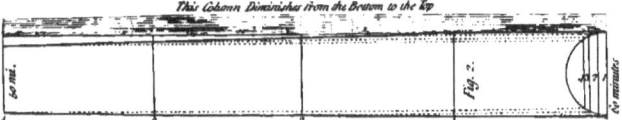

When Columns are fluted divide the Round or Circumference into 96 parts give three to a Flute and one to a Fillet.

Diminish the Staves of the Columns on the Faces before they are Glued together, this is a very safe and sure way for making the Column.

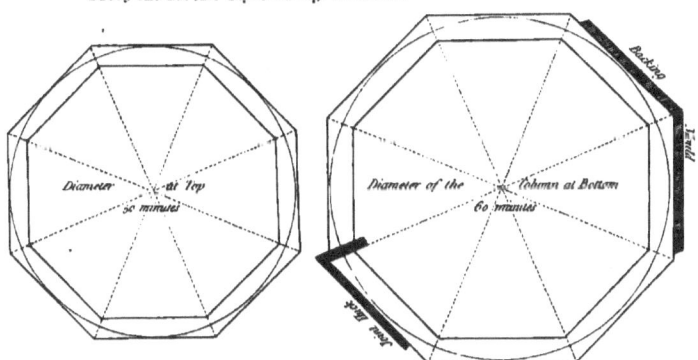

When Pilasters are Fluted divide the Breadth or Diameter into 20 parts give one to a Fillet and three to a Flute.

The Impost are twelfth Part of the Height from the Floor to the Springing of the Arch, or the Impost may be one eighteenth Part of the Height at Pleasure

Entablature for Doors Windows &c.
with all the Measures figured for Practice at Large.

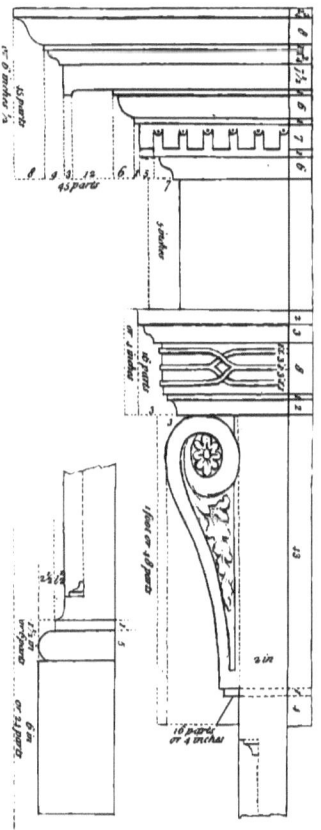

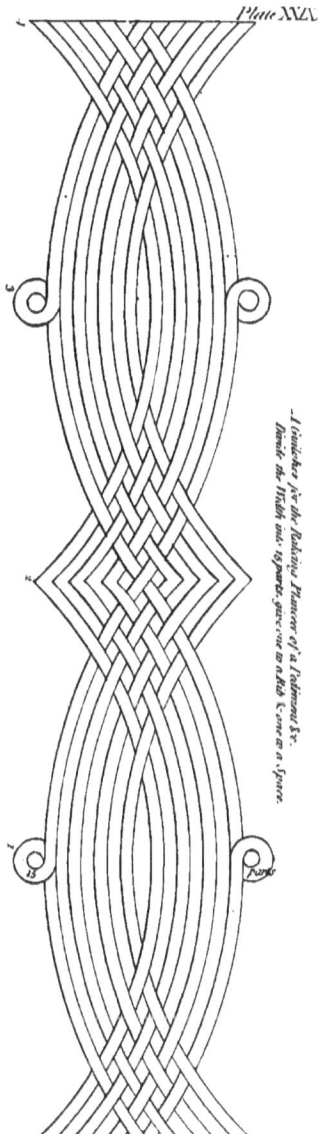

A similitude for the Releving Pattern of a Patterned &c.
Divide the Width into 18 parts, give one to each Turne or a Space.

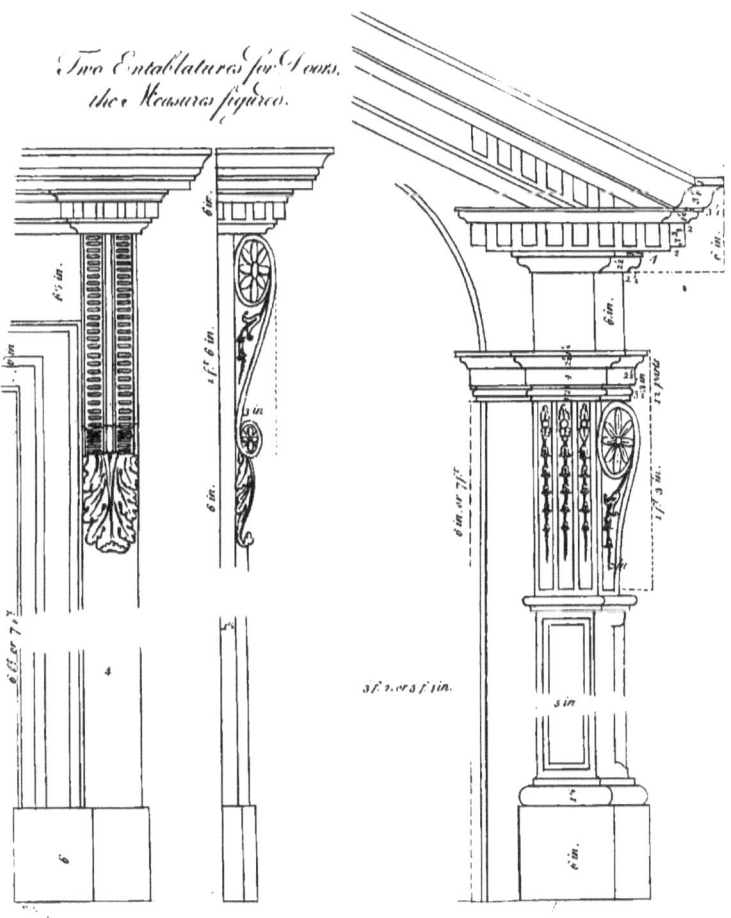

Plate XXX.

Two Entablatures for Doors, the Measures figured.

Frontispieces for Doors

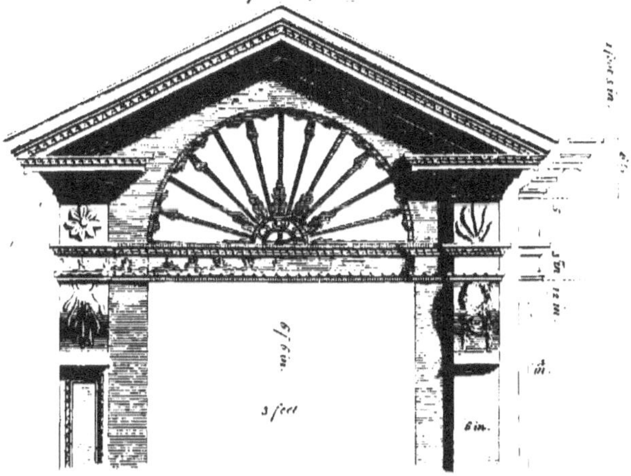

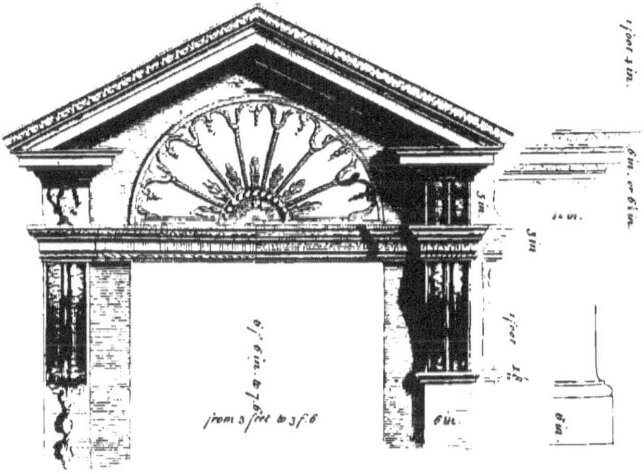

Plate XXVI.

Designs for Door Cases.

3 feet

4 in.

from 3 feet to 3 f 6

4 in   8 in

Plate XXVII.

Plate XXXIV.

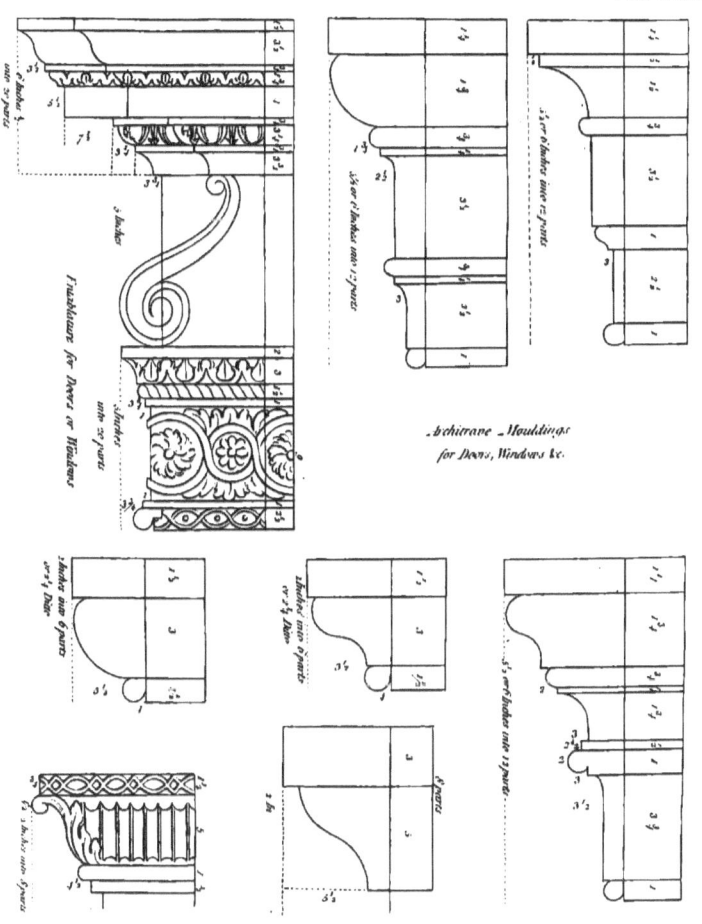

Architrave Mouldings
for Doors, Windows &c.

Plate XXXV.

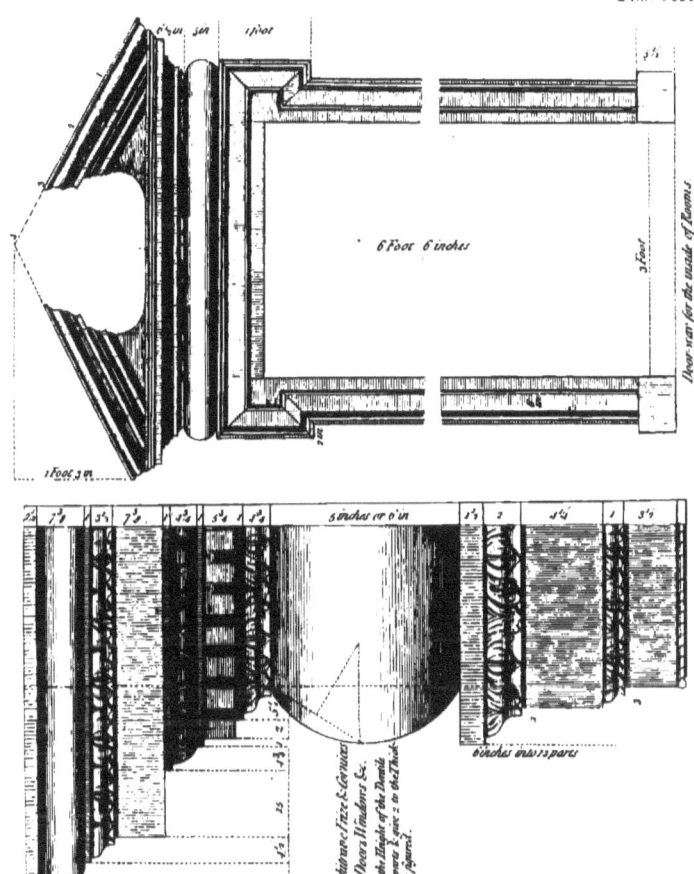

6 Foot 6 inches

3 Feet

Door way for the inside of Rooms

1 Foot 3 in.

1 Foot

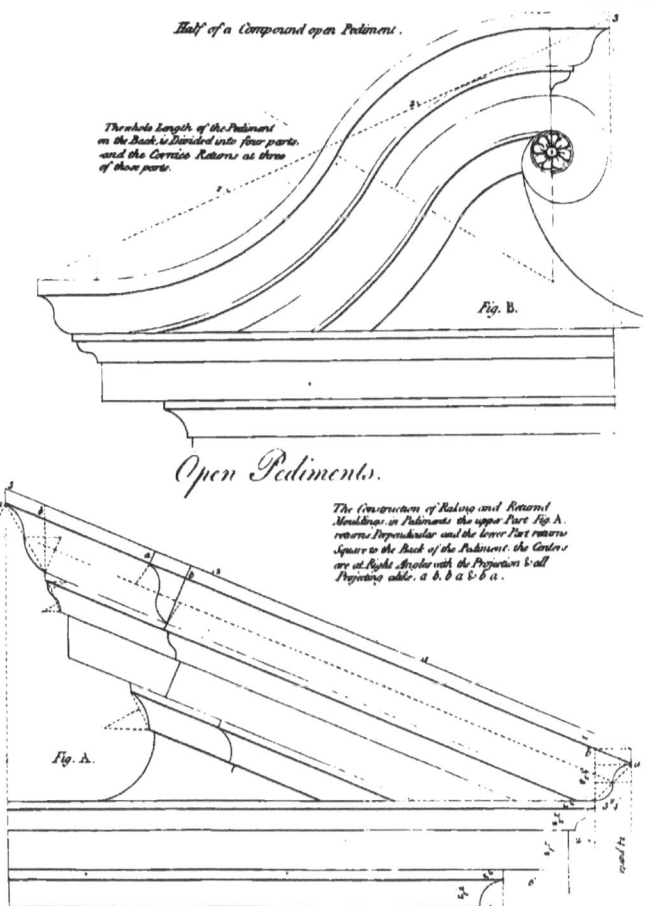

Plate XXXVI.

Half of a Compound open Pediment.

The whole Length of the Pediment on the Back, is Divided into four parts, and the Cornice Returns as three of those parts.

Fig. B.

Open Pediments.

The Construction of Raking and Returned Mouldings in Pediments. the upper Part Fig. A. returns Perpendicular and the lower Part returns Square to the Back of the Pediment. the Centers are at Right Angles with the Projection & all Projecting able. a b. b a & b a.

Fig. A.

Plate XXXVII.

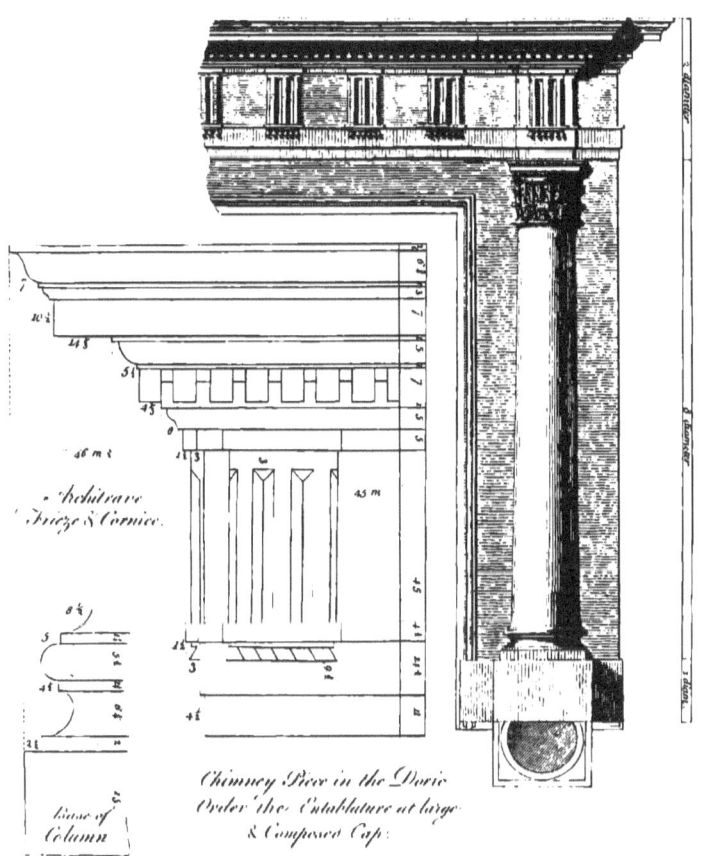

Architrave
Frieze & Cornice.

Base of
Column

Chimney Piece in the Doric
Order the Entablature at large
& Composed Cap.

Plate XXXVIII.

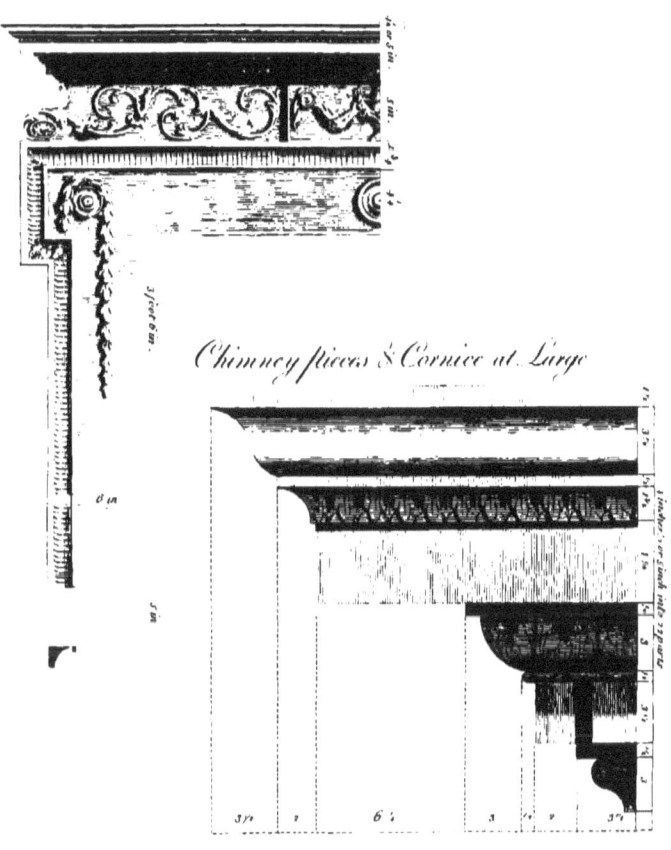

Chimney pieces & Cornice at Large

Plate XXIX.

Two Chimney Pieces with open Pediment, Glass or Picture frames ornamented.

Plate XL.

Two Designs for Chimneys with Caryattic Figures.

Cornice at large.

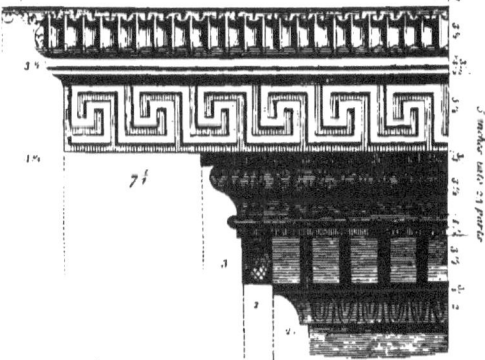

Plate XLI.

Two Designs for Chimney Pieces.

Plate XLII.

*Two Designs for Chimneys,
with their Mouldings at large.*

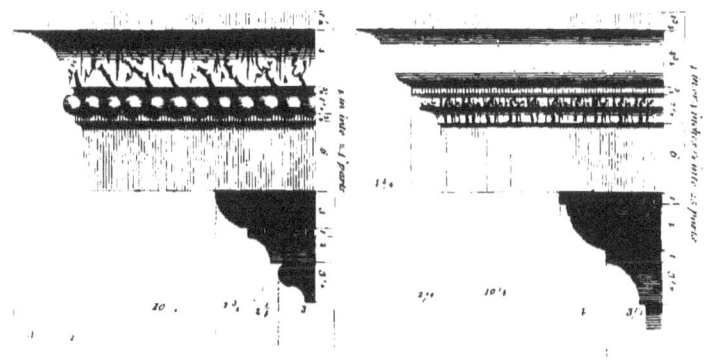

Place XLIII.

Two Designs for Chimney-Pieces.

Plate XLIV.

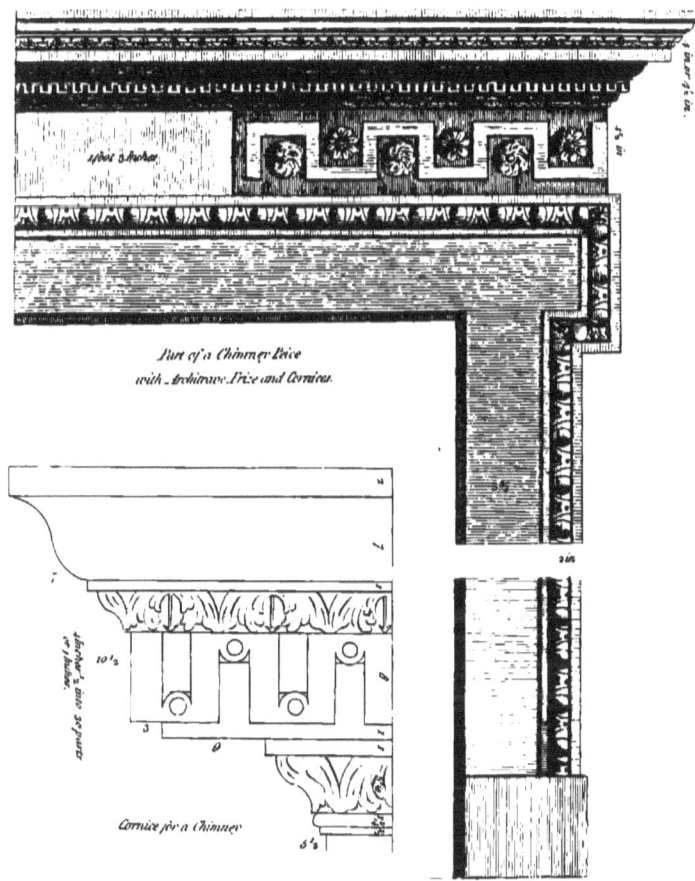

Part of a Chimney Piece
with Architrave Frize and Cornices.

Cornice for a Chimney

Plate XLV

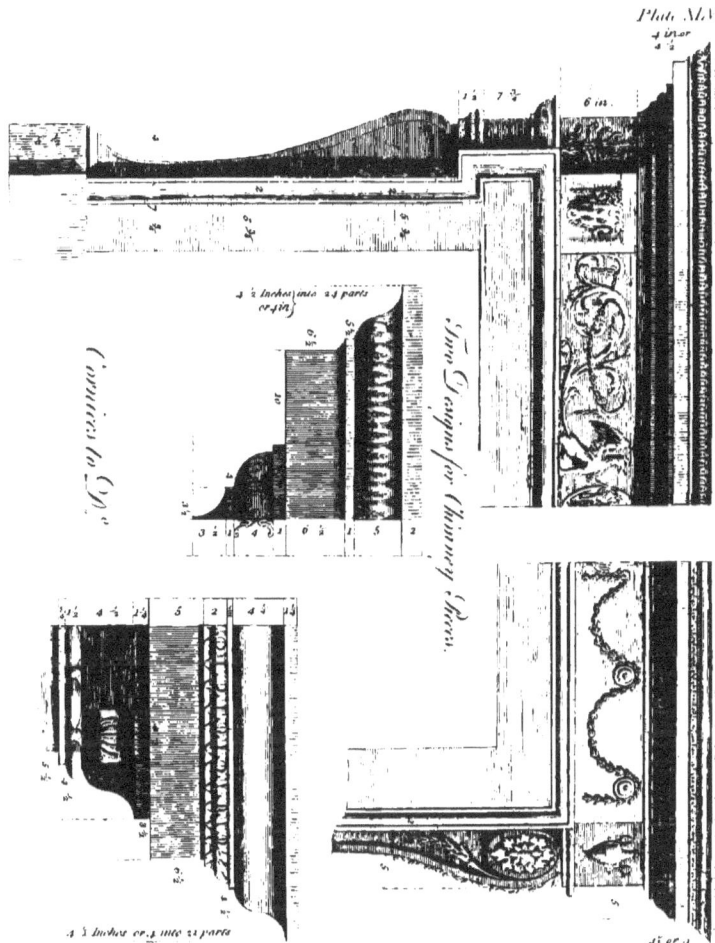

Two Designs for Chimney Pieces.

Cornice Pt:

Plate XLVI.

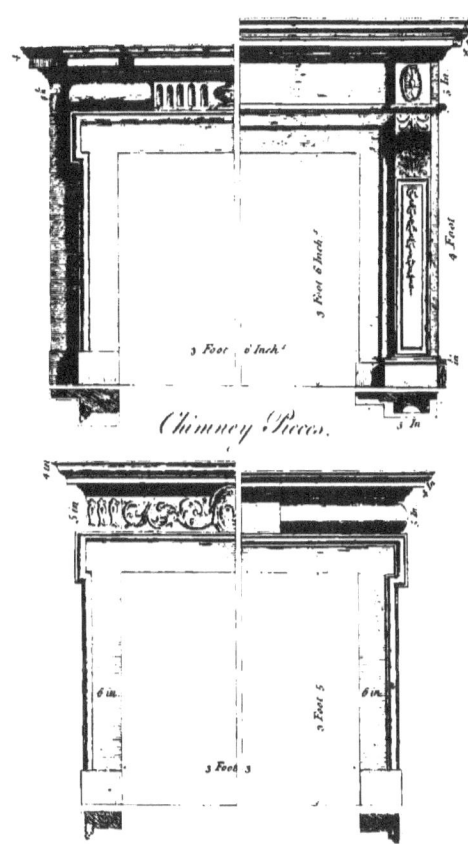

Chimney Pieces.

Plate XLVII.

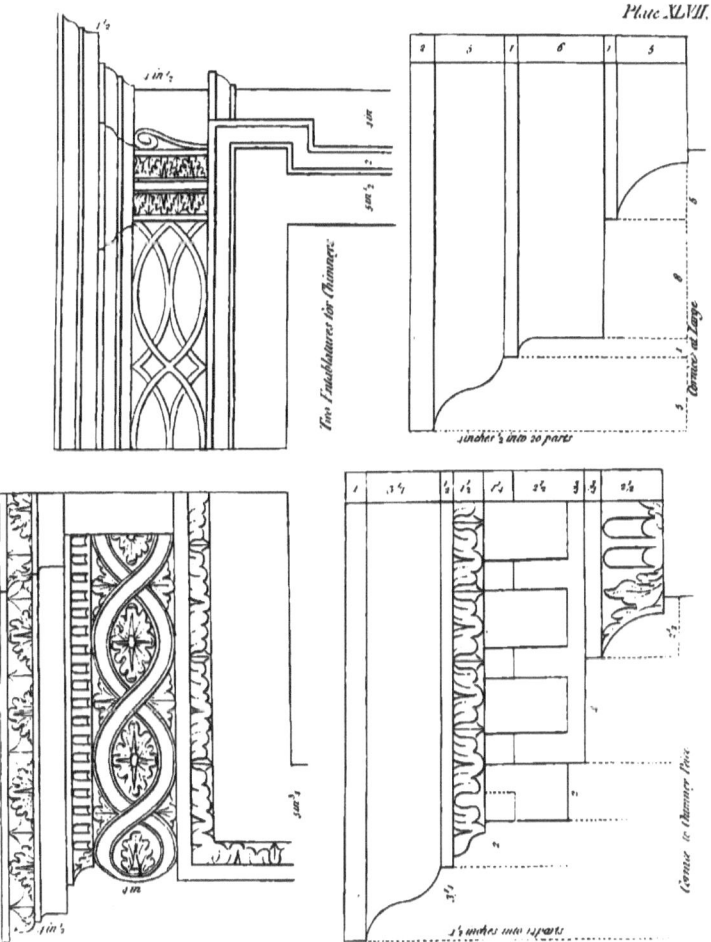

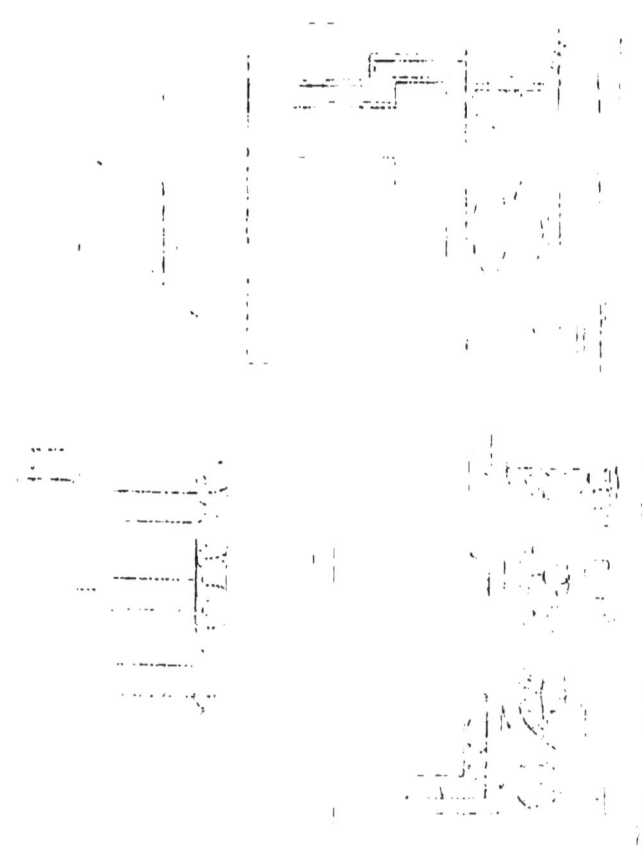

Plate XLVIII.

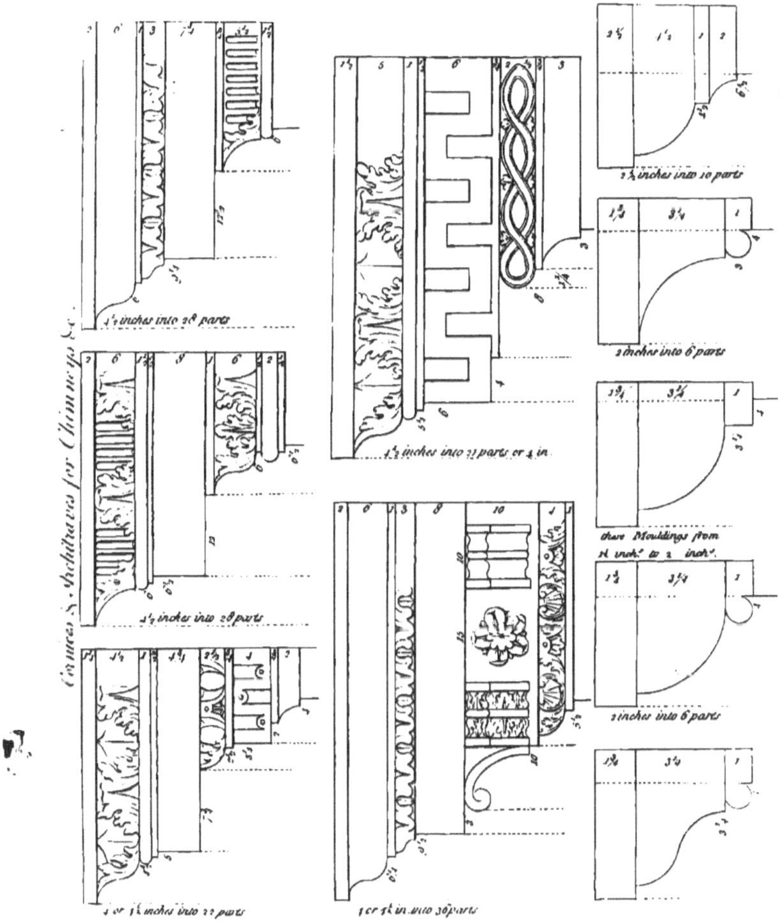

Cornices & Architraves for Chimneys &c.

1½ inches into 28 parts

1½ inches into 22 parts or 4 in.

1½ inches into 28 parts

4 or 3½ inches into 22 parts

4 or 3½ in. into 28 parts

2½ inches into 10 parts

2 inches into 6 parts

these Mouldings from 1½ inch to 2 inch.

2 inches into 6 parts

Plate XLIX.

Mouldings for Looking Glass or Picture Frames.

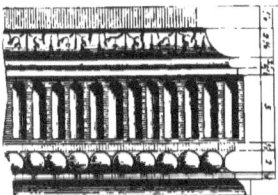

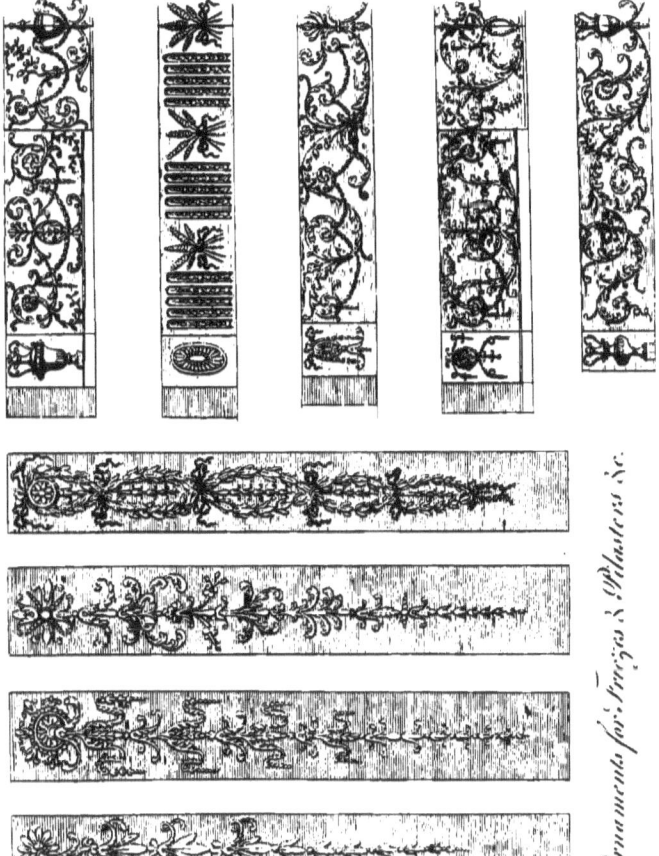

Plate L.

Ornaments for Freizes & Pilasters &c.

Plate LL.

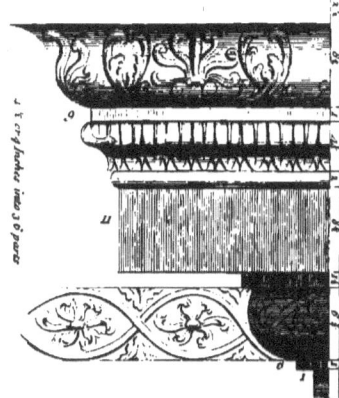

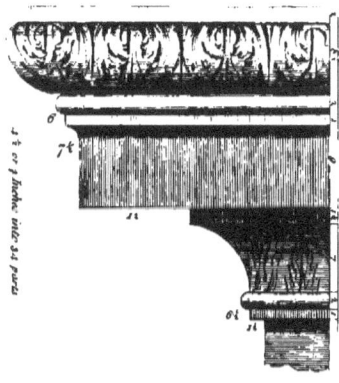

Cornices for Chimney Caps Doors or Windows &c.

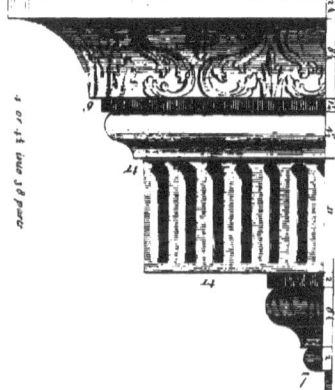

Plate LII.

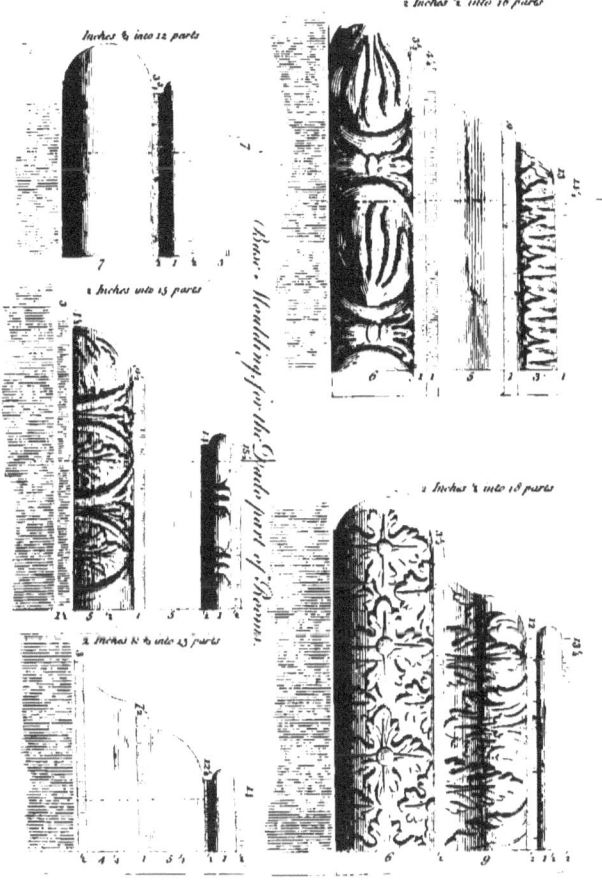

Inches ⅔ into 12 parts

2 Inches ½ into 18 parts

2 Inches into 15 parts

2 Inches ½ into 18 parts

2 Inches ½ into 15 parts

Ornamented Moulding for the Shaded part of Cornices.

Plate LIII.

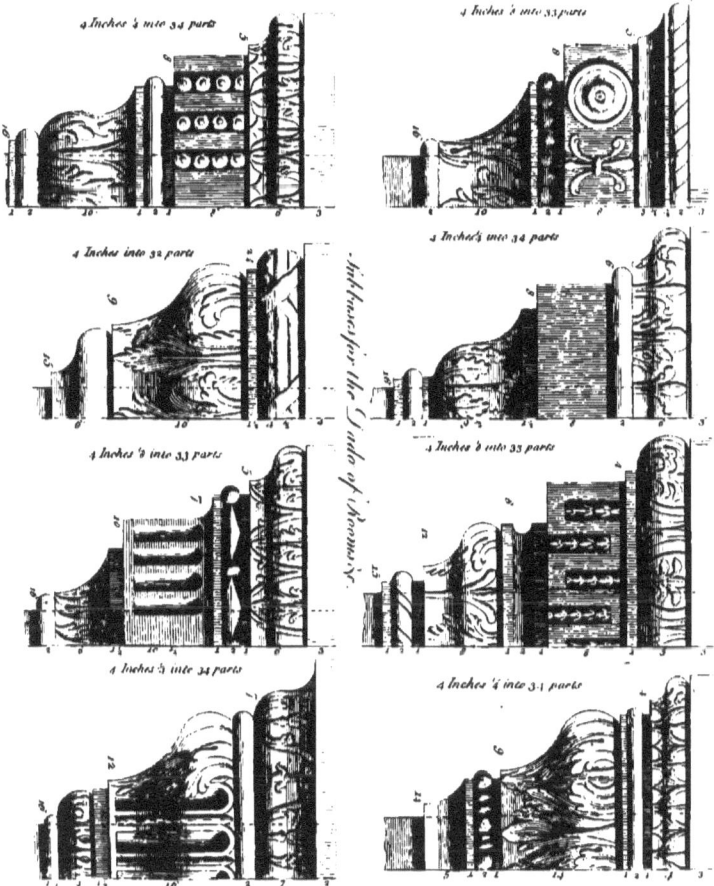

4 Inches ½ into 34 parts

4 Inches ½ into 33 parts

4 Inches into 32 parts

4 Inches ½ into 34 parts

4 Inches ½ into 33 parts

4 Inches ½ into 33 parts

4 Inches ½ into 34 parts

4 Inches ½ into 34 parts

Plate LIV.

Base & Sub-base for Rooms.

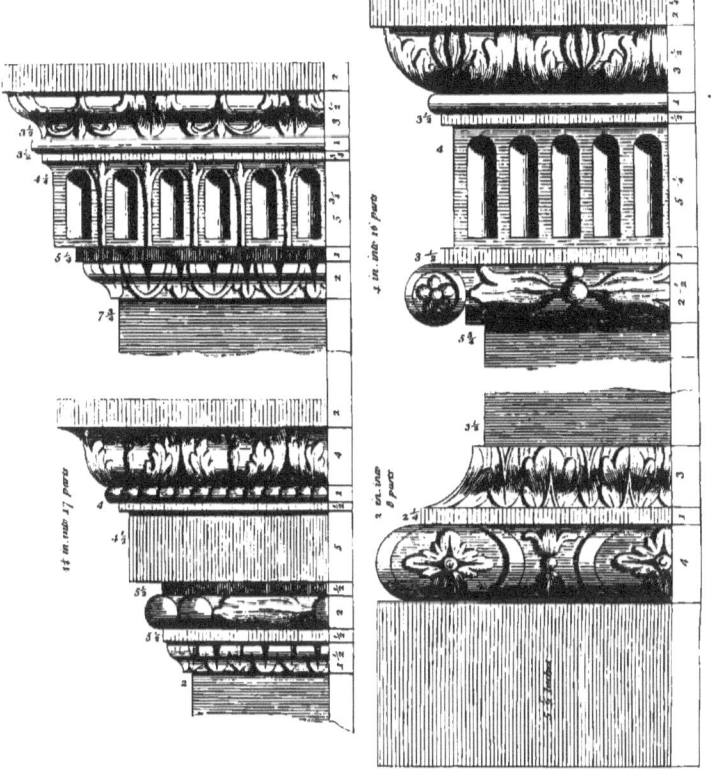

Plate IV.

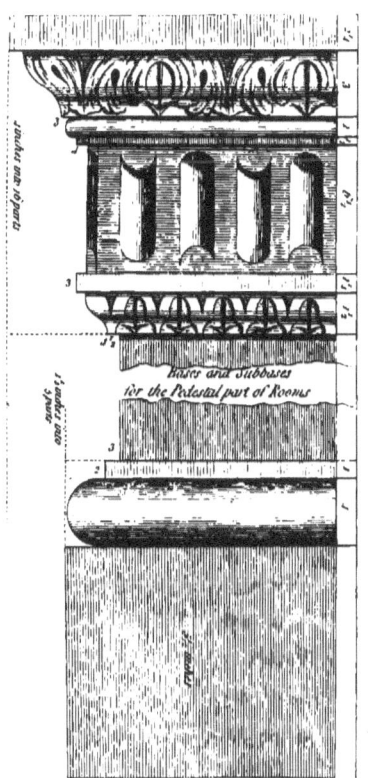

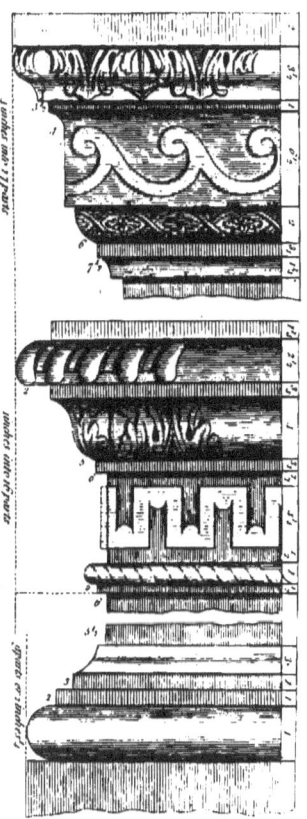

Bases and Subbases
for the Pedestal part of Rooms

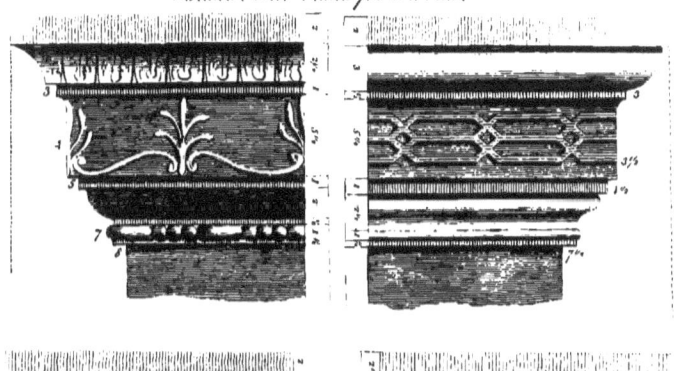

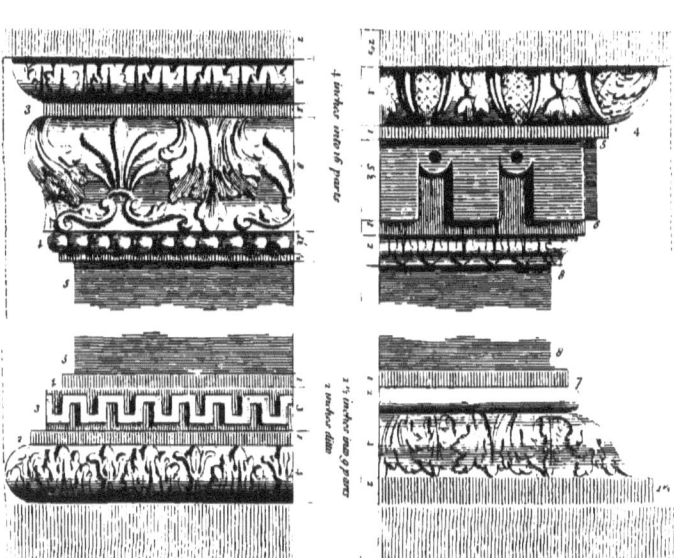

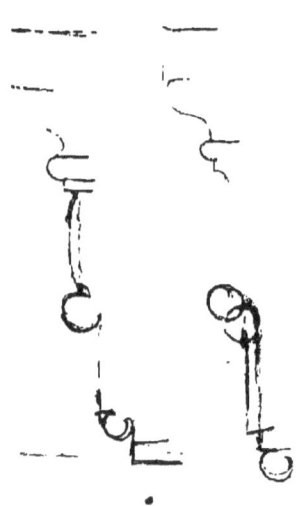

Plate LVII.

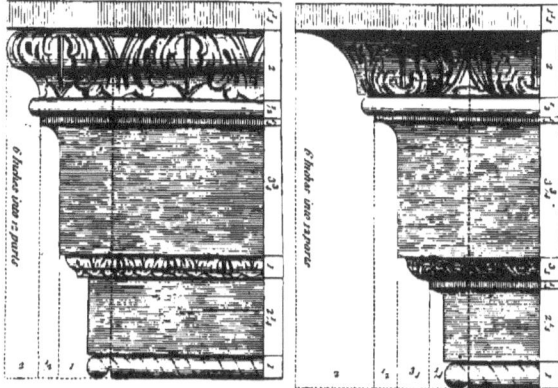

Architraves for Doors Windows &c. at large.

Plate LVIII.

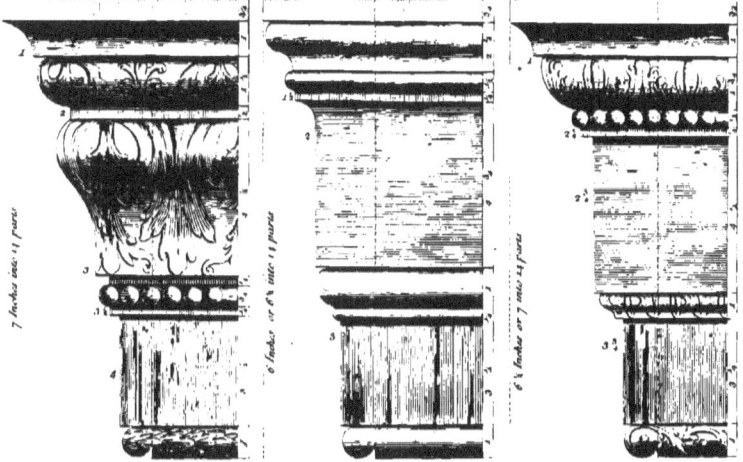

Architraves for Doors Windows &c.

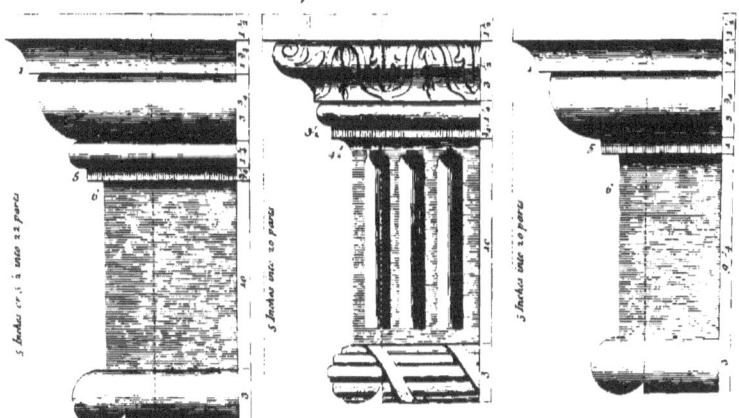

Plate LIX

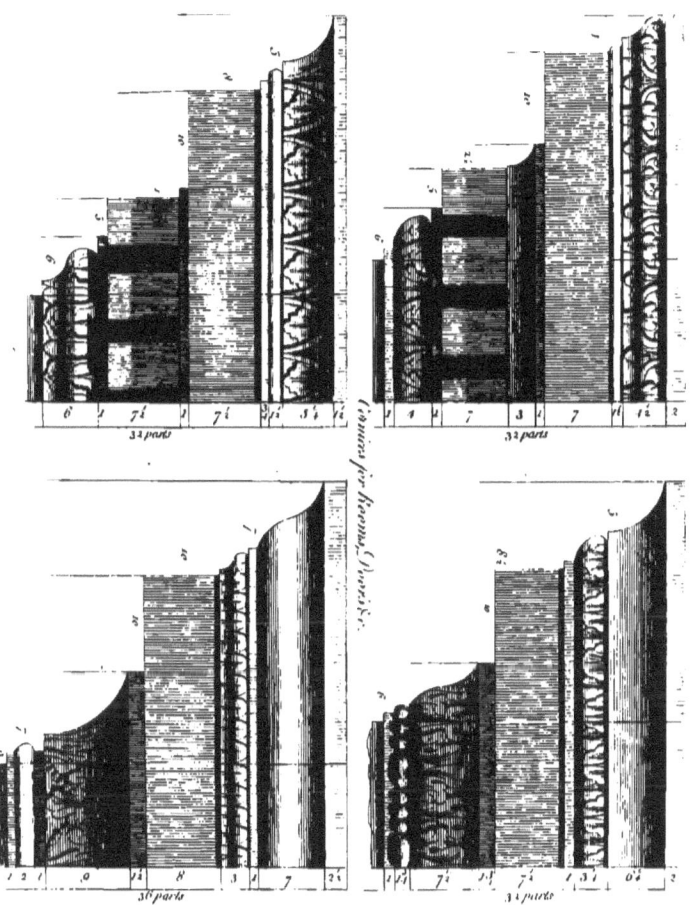

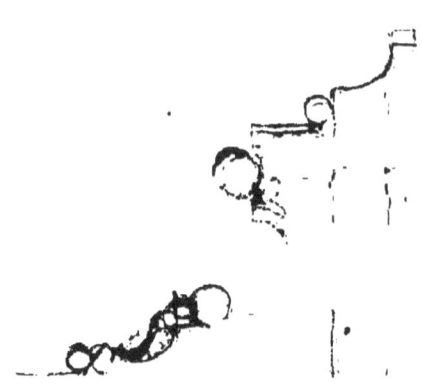

Plate LX.

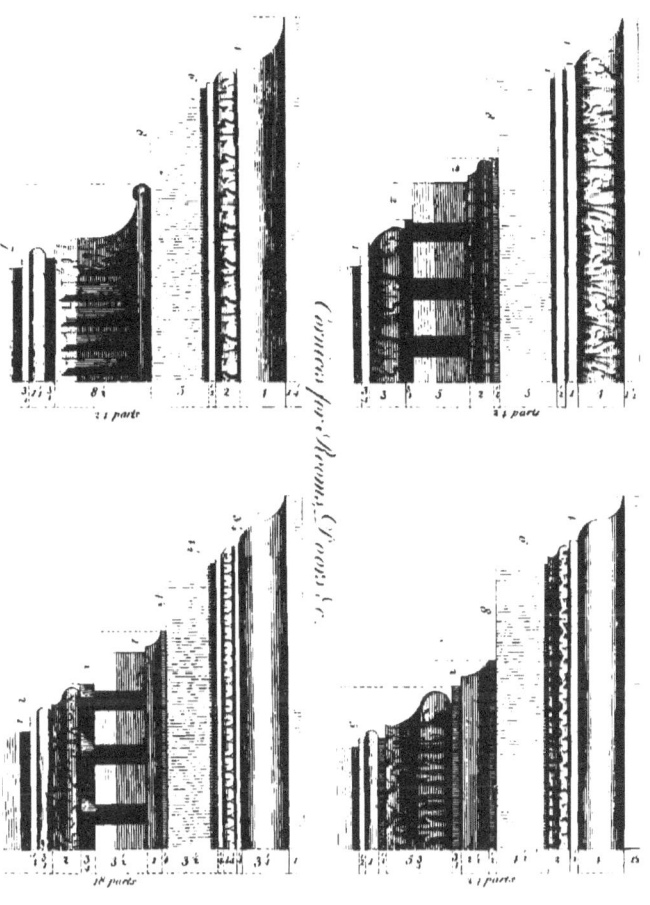

For Rooms 18 part of the whole height. For Doors from 6 to 7 inches.
For Stairways from 4 inches to 4½.

Cornices for Rooms &c Doors &c

2 1 parts

2 ½ parts

18 parts

4 1 parts

Plate LXI.

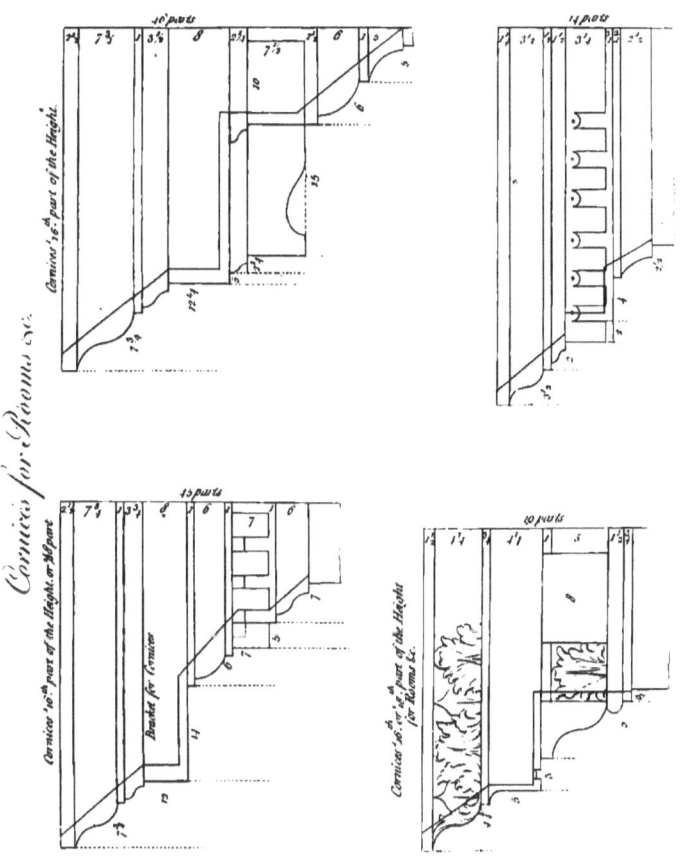

Cornices for Rooms &c.

Plate LXII.

Two Designs

for Ceilings.

Plate LXIII

Two Designs for Ceilings.

Plate LXIV.

Frets & Guiloches.

Plate LXV.

Frets.

Plate LXVI

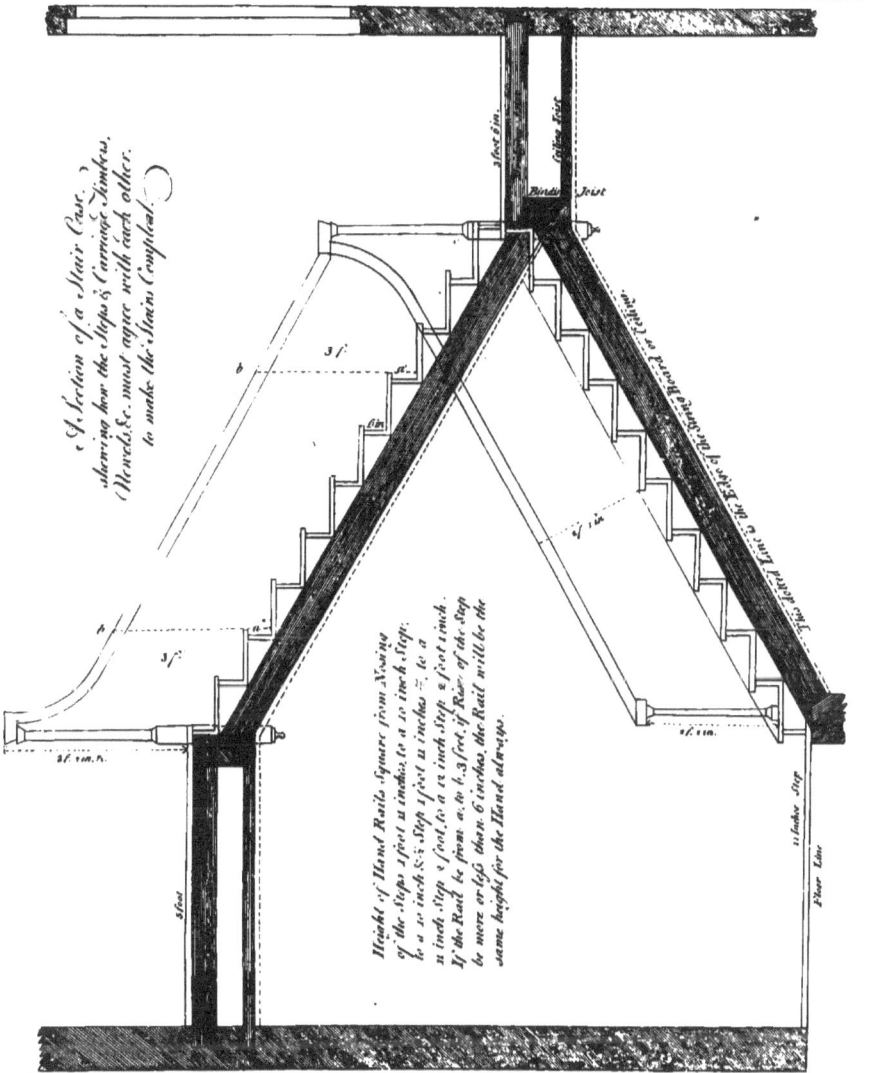

A Section of a Stair Case,
shewing how the Steps & Carriage Timbers,
Newels, &c. must agree with each other,
to make the Stairs compleat.

Height of Hand Rails Square from Nosing
of the Steps 2 feet 11 inches, to a 10 inch Step;
to a 11 inch 8½ Step 2 feet 11 inches; to a
12 inch Step 2 foot, to a 12 inch Step 2 foot 1 inch.
If the Rail be from a, to b, 3 feet, if Rise of the Step
be more or less than 6 inches, the Rail will be the
same height for the Hand always.

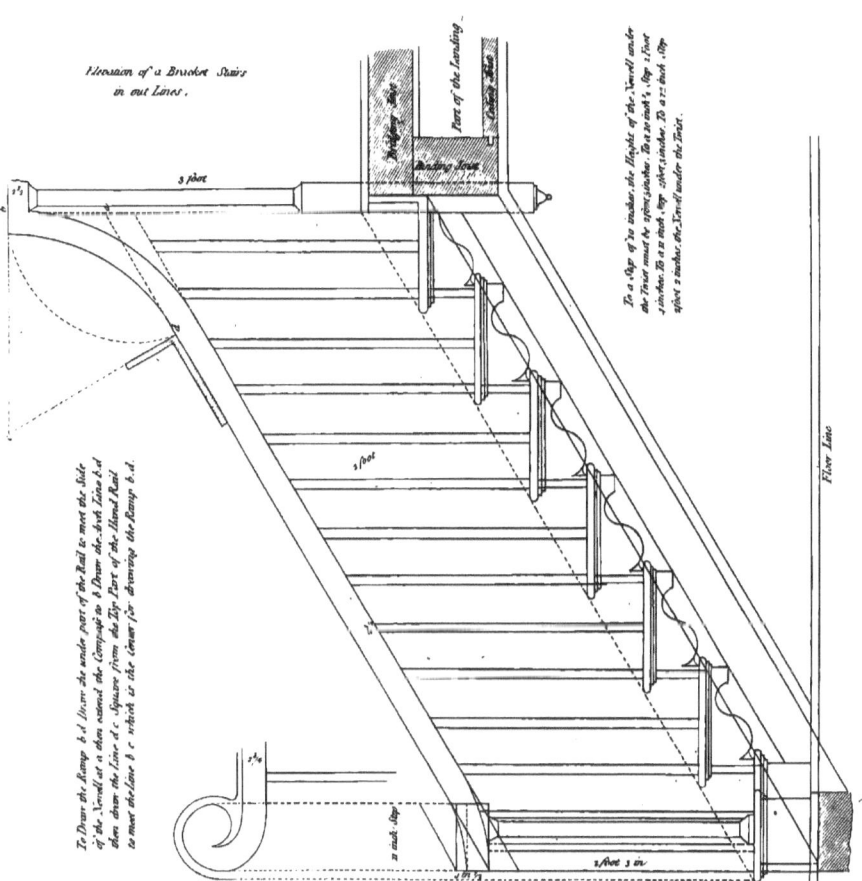

Plate LXVII.

Elevation of a Bracket Stairs
in out Lines.

Part of the Landing.

Carriage Piece

Bearing Iron

3 feet

To Draw the Ramp b d Draw the under part of the Rail to meet the Side of the Newell at a then extend the Compass to b Draw the Arch Line b d then draw the Line d c square from the Top Part of the Hand Rail to meet the Line b c which is the center for drawing the Ramp b d.

To a Step of 3½ inches the Height of the Newell under the Twist must be 2 feet 3 inches. To a 10 inch step 2 feet 1 inch. To a 12 inch step 2 feet 1 inch. To a 15 inch step 2 inches the Newell under the Twist.

Floor Line

3 feet

2 feet 3 in.

Plate LXVIII.

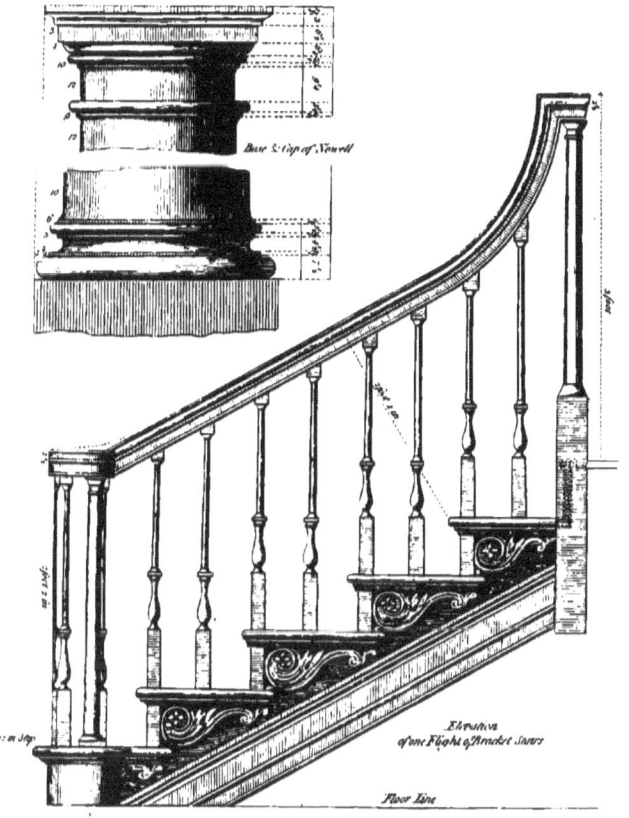

Base & Top of Newell

Elevation
of one Flight of Bracket Stairs

Floor Line

To face P L A T E LXIX.

To draw the Plan and Scroll of a twift Rail for a Stair-Cafe.

D RAW a Circle equal to the Breadth of two Steps, and divide it into
eight Parts, then draw a Circle round the Centre five Inches Diameter,
as 2, 3, then draw the Line *e*, *f*, and fet one Foot of the Compafs at *e*,
and draw the Arch Line 7, o, which muft be divided into eight Parts, and
draw Lines from *e*, thro' each eighth Part to the Line 1, 2, 3, 4, 5, &c.
then fet the Compafs in the Centre of the Scroll, and draw the dotted Lines
from 1 on the Scale to 1 on the Edge of the Rail, and from 2 to 2 on the
Edge of the Rail, and fo for all the Reft to each eighth Part of the Circle,
which gives the outer Edge of the Rail.

To find the Centre for drawing each eighth Part, fet one Foot of the
Compafs in the Centre of the Scroll, and take the Diftance to *f*, with the
fame Radius; fet the Foot at *e*, and make a Mark at *c*, and with the fame
Radius fet one Foot at 1 on the Edge of the Rail, and bifect the former
Stroke at *c*, which is the Centre for the firft eighth Part, then take from
the Centre of the Scroll to 1 on the Scale, and fet one Foot at 1 on the
Edge of the Rail, make a Mark in the Eye and move the Compafs to 2 on
on the Edge of the Rail, and bifect the former Stroke, that is the Centre
for the fecond eighth Part, and fo on for all the Reft. The Centre for the
Front of Rifer and Nofing of Step are the black Dots, one fifth Part from
the Rail to the Nofing of the Step without the other Centre; the Pieces
which make the twift Part of the Rail are *d*, *e*, *b*, on the raking Mould
the Twift begins at *a* on the Edge of the Rail, and Ends at three on ditto,
the remaining Part is level; the lower Part of the Scroll from 2 is cut out
of a Parallel Piece, as reprefented by *g* on the Newel, &c.

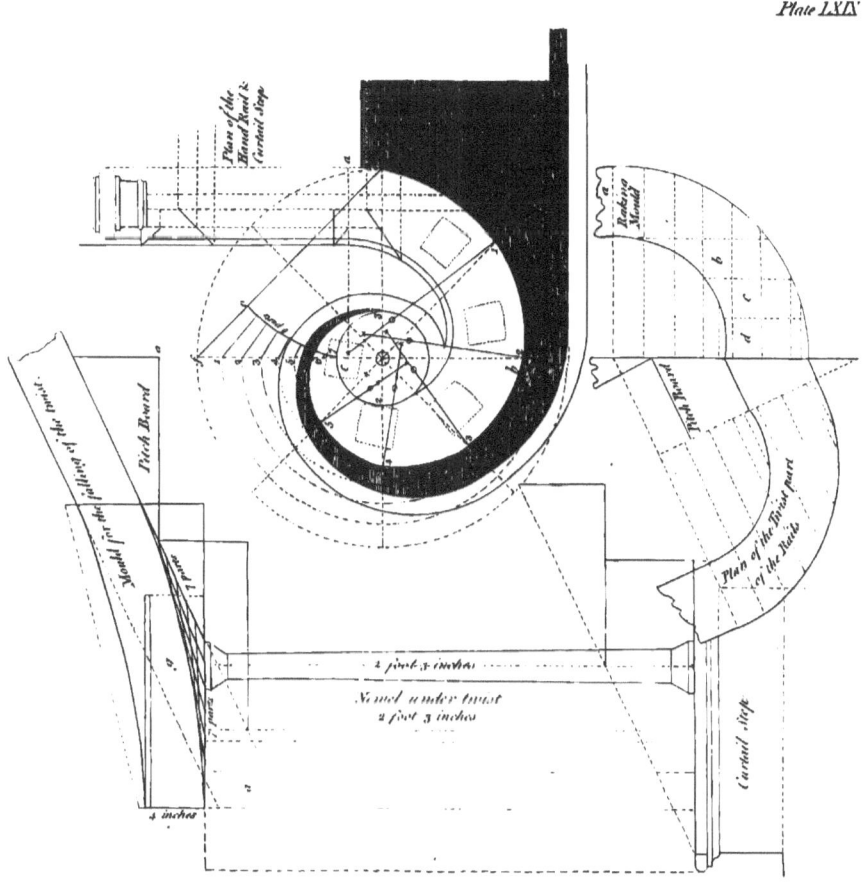

Plate LXIV

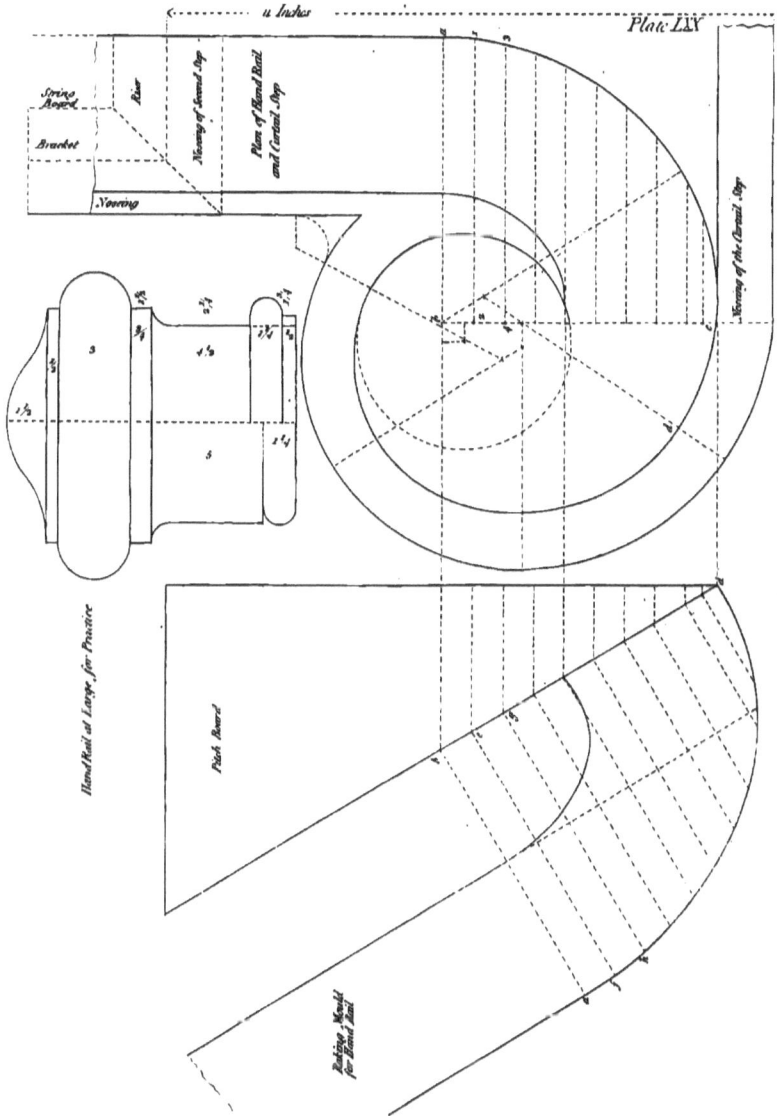

Plate LIX

11 Inches

String Board

Bracket

Riser

Nosing of Second Step

Plan of Hand Rail and Curtail Step

Nosing

Nosing of the Curtail Step

Hand Rail at Large for Practice

Plank Board

Raking Mould for Hand Rail

Plate LXVI.

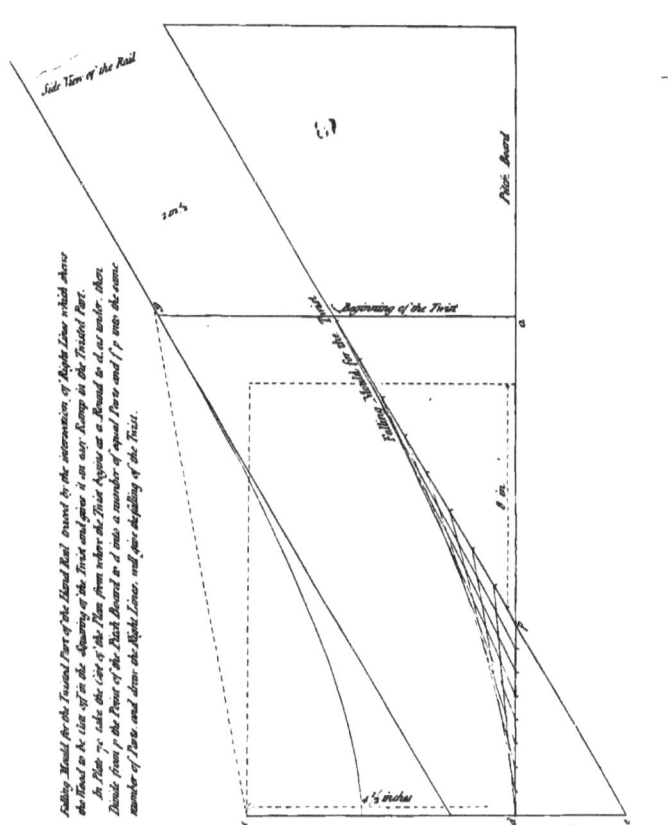

Side View of the Rail

Point Board

Beginning of the Twist

Falling Mould for the Twist

5 ½ inches

Falling Mould for the Twisted Part of the Hand Rail. Drawn by the intersection of Right Lines which show the Hand to be slee off in the squaring of the Twist and gives it an easy Ramp in the Twisted Part.

In Plate 75. take the line of the Plan from under the Twist square as a Round to d as under, then Divide from f the Point of the Point Board to d into a number of equal Parts and f p into the same number of Parts and draw the Right Lines, and gives stiffning of the Twist.

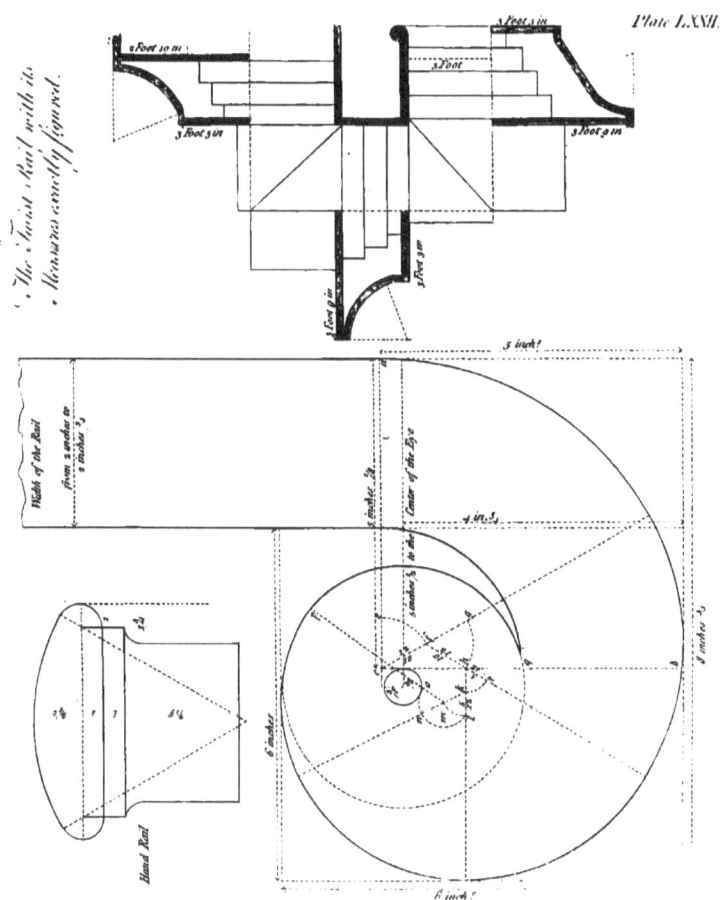

The Twist Rail with its Members correctly figured.

Plate LXXII.

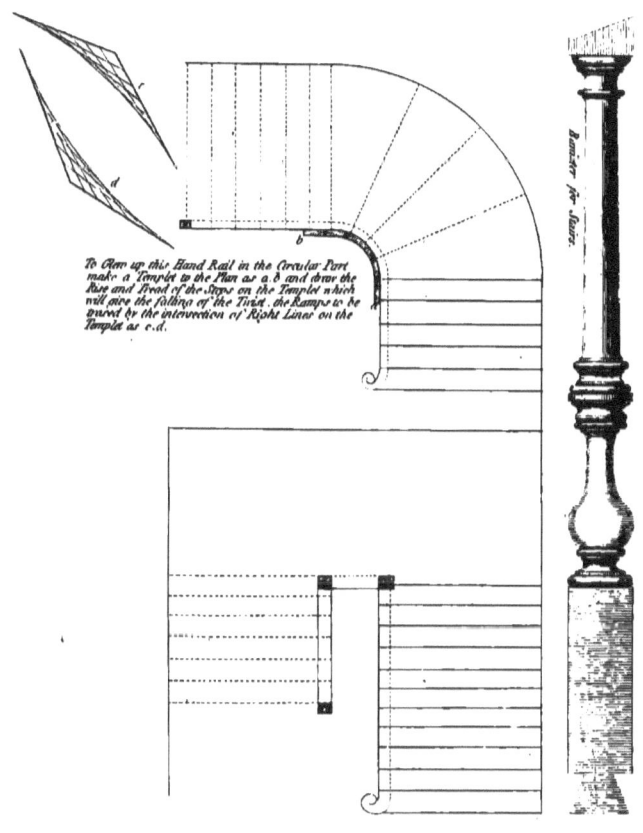

Plate LXVII.

Two Plans for Stair Cases.

To Glew up this Hand Rail in the Circular Part
make a Templet to the Plan as a.b and draw the
Rise and Tread of the Steps on the Templet which
will give the falling of the Twist. the Ramps to be
mixed by the intersection of Right Lines on the
Templet as c.d.

Banisters for Stairs.

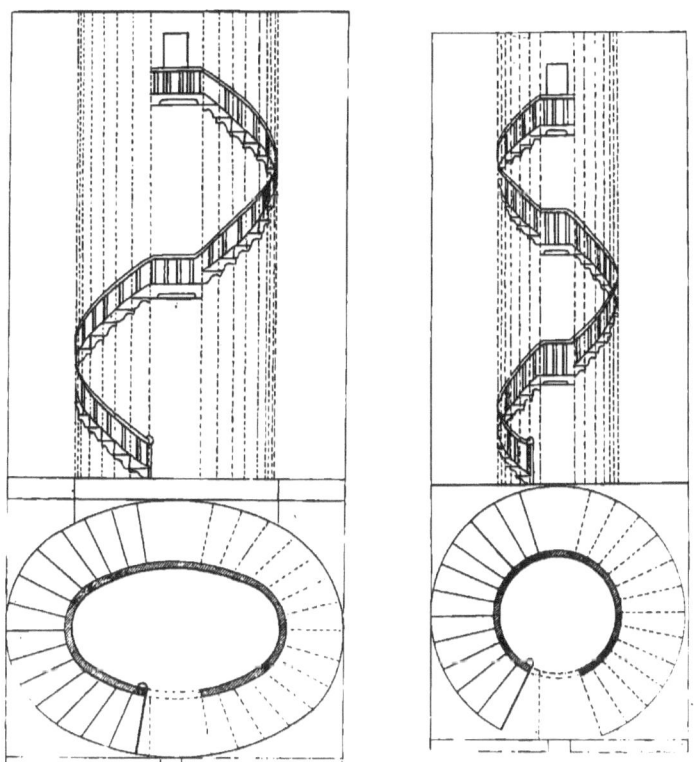

To be lighted by a Dome or Cone Lanthorn at the top, if placed in the middle of
a Building. If on the outside may be lighted by Windows in the Wall at each landing.
To make the Hand-rail make a Templet or Cylinder to the well hole or open of the
Rail, draw the tread & use of each Step on the Cylinder, and that will give the falling
of the Rail, which is to be allowed in thickness bent round the Cylinder, then the
Rail will come off ready squared, this is a very sure way to make the Rail.

Plate LXXV

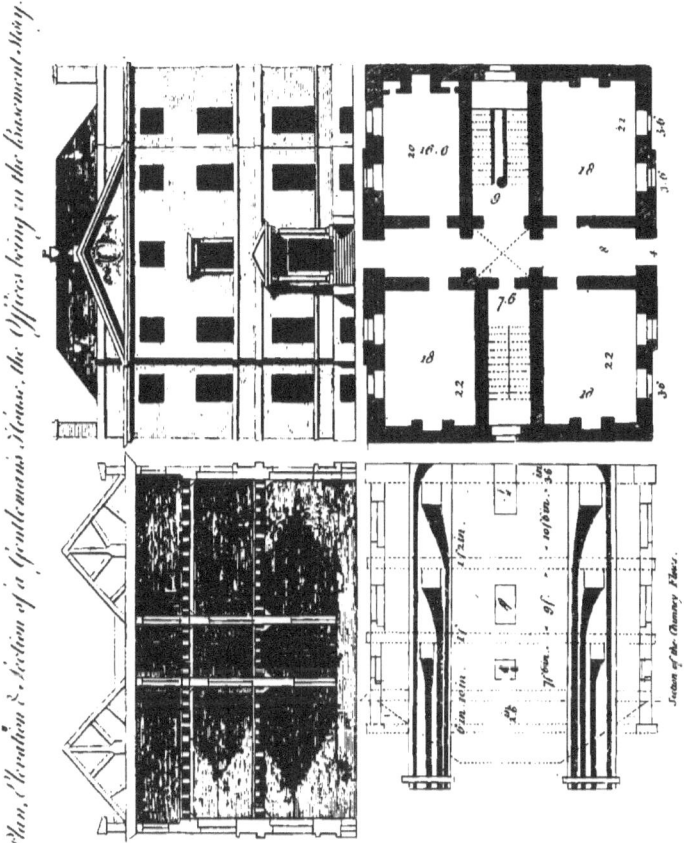

Plan, Elevation & Section of a Gentleman's House, the Offices being in the Basement Story.

Plate LXXVI.

Plan and Elevation of a Gentleman's House.

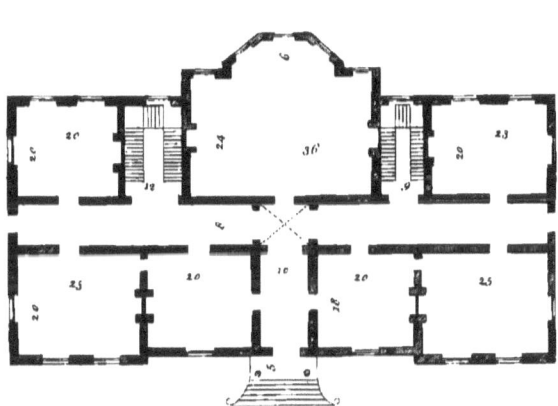

Plate LXXVII.

Plan & Elevation of a Gentlemans House.

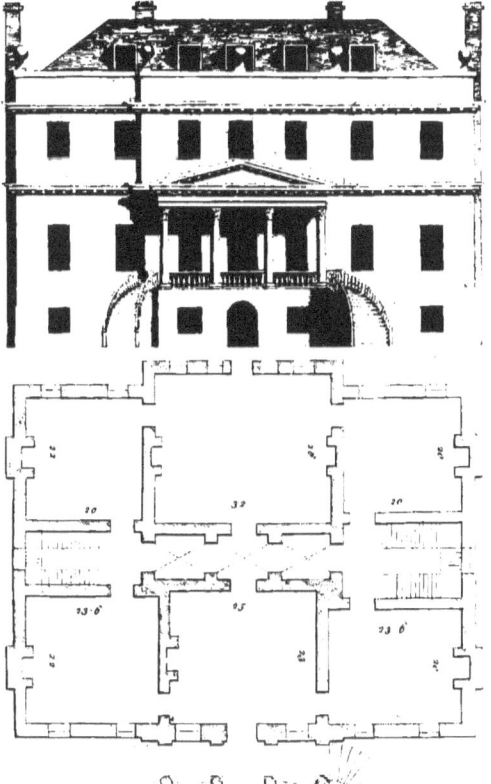

Plate LXXVIII

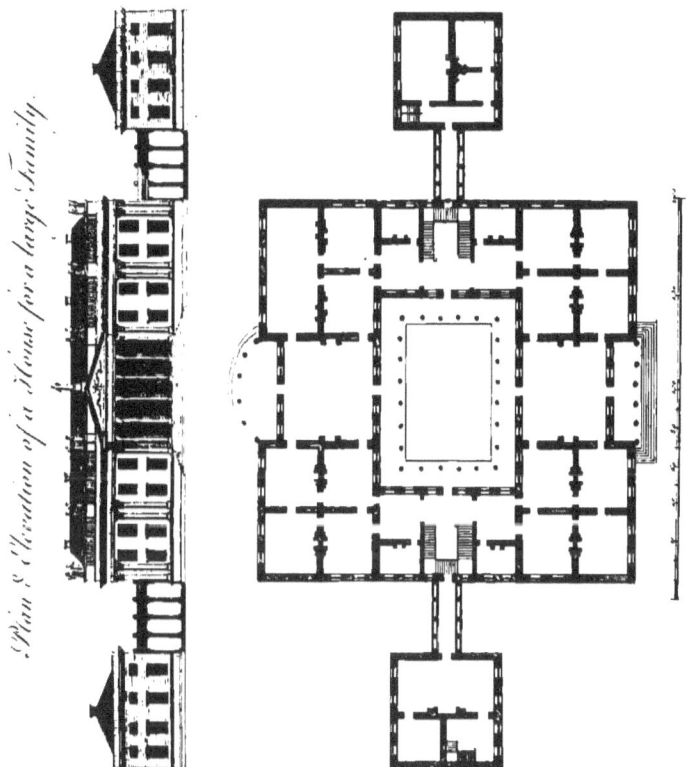

Plan & Elevation of a House for a large Family.

Plate LXXIX

Plan and Elevation for a Dwelling-House.

Front & Profile of the Plaster-Tray & Cornice at large for Green-House.

Plan and Elevation of a Green-House intended on stone Pillars.

Plate LXIX.

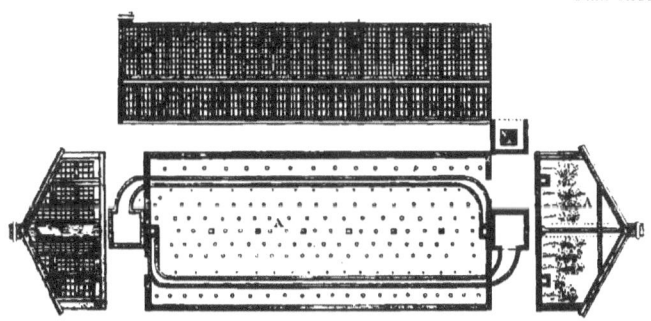

Two Plans, Elevations and Sections for Stoves or Hot Houses
for Pines, Fruit Trees, Strawberrys &c.

The Plan and Section A is for Fruit Trees.

The Plan B, for Pines; the Flues in this Plan run one over another as may be seen in the
Section. There are Five Flues at each End and a Walk all round.

The Flues in the Plan A. Run on the Surface and are single Flues.

The Front Roof and Ends Glass as the Elevation of the Plan A.

The Width of each House is 16 Feet the Length at Pleasure from 40 to 50 Feet, or more at pleasure.

Plate LXXXI

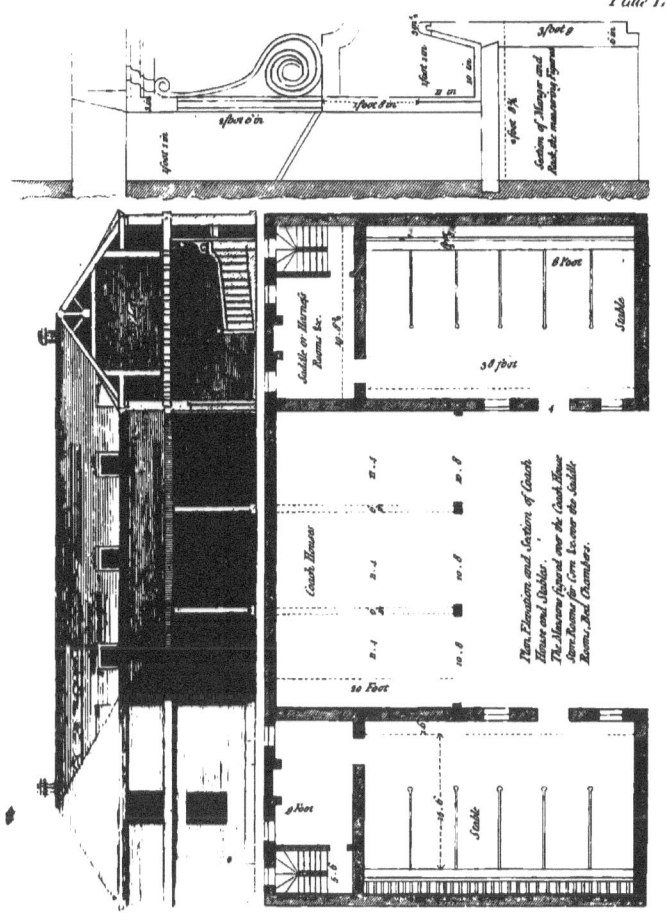

Plan, Elevation and Section of Coach
House and Stables.
The Numbers figured over the Coach House
shew Rooms for Corn &c over the Saddle
Rooms, Bed Chambers.

Section of Manger and
Rack &c. measuring Figures

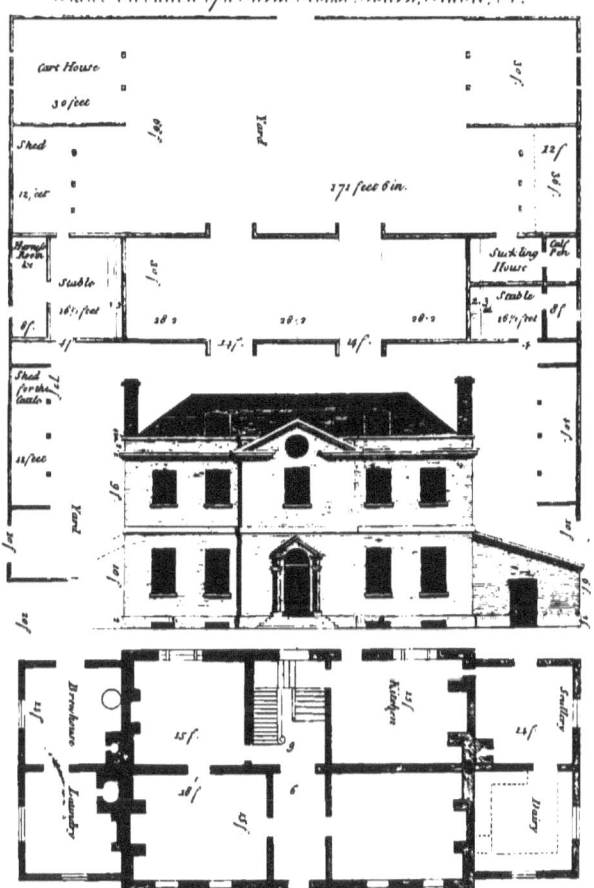

Plate LXXIII.

Plan, Elevation & Section &c. of a Farm-house Barns, Stables &c.

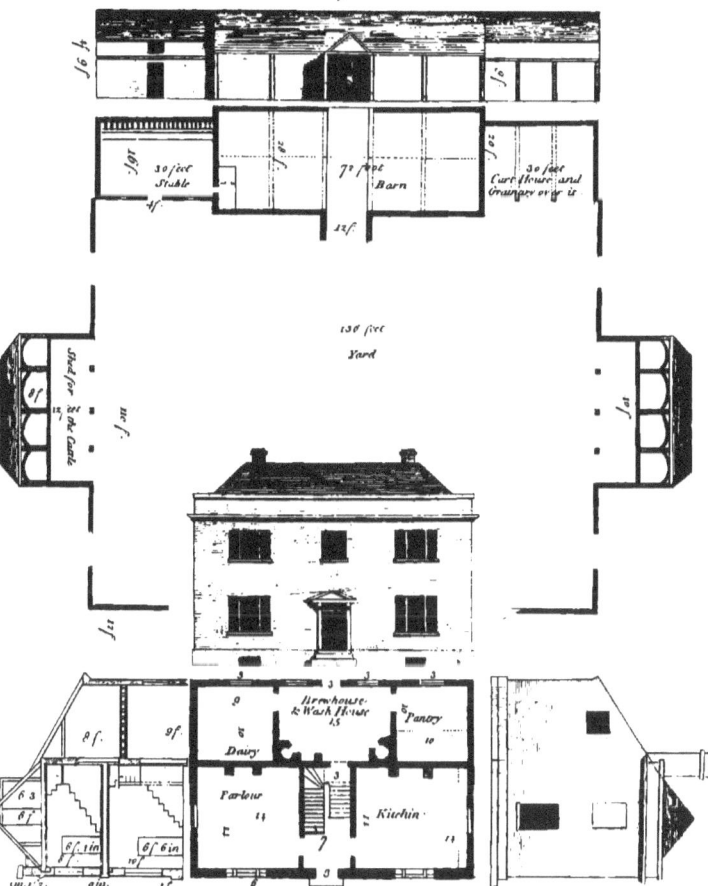

B O O K S printed for and fold by *I. TAYLOR.*

1 THE Carpenter's Treafure; a Collection of Defigns for Temples, with their Plans, Gates, Doors, Rails, and Bridges, in the Gothic Tafte; with the Centres at large, for ftriking Gothic Curves and Mouldings; and fome Specimens of Rails, in the Chinefe Tafte: Forming a complete Syftem for rural Decorations. Neatly engraved on fixteen Plates, from the original Drawings of N. WALLIS, Architect   2s. 6d.

2. A Book of Ornaments in the Palmyrene Tafte, containing upwards of fixty new Defigns for Ceilings, Pannels, Pateras, and Mouldings: with the Raffle Leaves at large: By N. WAL-LIS, Architect, elegantly engraved on 12 Plates.   4s. 6d. fewed.

3. The Compleat Modern Joiner, or a Collection of original Defigns in the prefent Tafte, for Chimney-Pieces and Door-Cafes, with their Mouldings and Enrichments at large; Frizes, Tablets, Ornaments for Pilafters, Bafes, Sub-bafes and Cornices for Rooms, &c. with a Table fhewing the Proportion of Chimnies, with their Entablatures, to Rooms of any Size.   By N. WALLIS, Architect.   8s. fewed, bound 10s.

Note, Both the above Books few'd in one, 12s. or 14s. bound.

4. A new Book of Ornaments, defigned by T. LAWS, Carver.   2s. fewed.

5. A new Book of Foliage, on ten Plates, for the Ufe of Learners, &c. By *H. Gerrard*.2s. fd.

6. The Gentleman and Tradefman's Compleat Affiftant, or the whole Art of Meafuring and Eftimating made Eafy; containing the Names and Prices of all Artificers Work in general, relating to Building, *viz.* Bricklayers, Carpenters, Joiners, Carvers, Plaifterers, Painters, Paviours, Smiths, &c.   3s. 6d. fewed, 4s. 6d. bound.

7. LANGLEY's Builder's Cheft-Book, or Key to the Five Orders of Architecture.   Second Edition, much improv'd.   3s. bound.

8. Fourteen Vafes from the Antique.   2s. fewed.

9. The Builder's Jewel. By B. LANGLEY.   4s. 6d. bound.

10. The Builder's Director, or Bench-Mate; on 184 Plates.   4s. bound.

11. HOPPUS's Practical Meafurer, greatly enlarged and improved, 2s. 6d. bound.

12. The Modern Gardener, or Univerfal Kallender; containing monthly Directions for all the Operations of Gardening; to be done either in the Kitchen, Fruit, Flower, or Pleafure Gardens: Illuftrated with 13 Plates, neatly engraved, of entire new Plans for Stoves, Green-houfes, &c.   By JAMES MEADER, late Gardener to the EARL of CHESTERFIELD.   4s. fewed, 5s. bd.

13. The Stove-Grate Maker's Affiftant, or a Treafury of Original and Fafhionable Defigns, for Bath-Stoves, Penfylvania-Stoves, fingle and double Standard Grates, Frets, &c. By W. GLOSSOP, Stove-Grate Maker.   Elegantly engraved on 24 Plates.   5s. fewed.

14. The Plan and Elevation (on two large Sheets) of that grand Structure *Mafra*, near *Lifbon*, the Palace of the King of *Portugal*, Price 6s.

15. A large Print of *Shoreditch*-Church.   3s.

16. A Print of *Greenwich* Church, 1s.

17. Health, an Effay on its Nature, Value, Uncertainty, Prefervation and beft Improvement. By B. GROSVENOR, D. D. 2s. 6d. bound.

18. *Le Beau's* Compendious French Teacher; to which are added, thirty-eight Letters of Commerce, in French, as Models to thofe who would chufe to form themfelves to the ufeful Style of Epiftolatory Correfpondence.   2s. bound.